# Journey to Glastonbury

*By Lawrence Compagna*

*First edition copyright 2019*

*Candco Publishing,*

*A Division of the Candco Corporation*

*ISBN: 978-1-947618-07-7*

D0721666

*After viewing the summer solstice at Stonehenge, a gray haired man finds himself five thousand miles away and ten years in the past. Armed with knowledge of the future, he believes that he has power to change the destiny of a young man and the girl he loves as they prepare to embark on a journey to fulfill a dream.*

*A haunting story of loss and redemption, Journey to Glastonbury is sure to move you in ways you don't expect.*

*Dedicated to Conrad and Madison*

## Table of Contents

"I don't want to play Glastonbury on the Sunday night in the pouring rain, which is what The Who did this year. I was watching it on the telly, and my kids were there. I'm on the phone saying 'it's awful'. They said it's really fun, but it didn't look fun to me."

- Mick Jagger, singer, the Rolling Stones

# June 21$^{st}$, 2023

# Prologue – Ten Years Later

*The summer solstice – Stonehenge, Amesbury, United Kingdom*

A middle-aged couple dance nearly naked on the grass field only twenty yards from the circle of stones. Under the clear moonlit sky their graying hair, long and unleashed, sways to the drum beat of a group of druids, one with bare knees under his tartan kilt. Behind me I see a crow, blacker than the warm night, screaming at them from the top of the biggest stone. Through the twilight, I can see that this bird is not alone. Others of his kind line the moss covered trilithons – two upright rocks with a flat one placed atop them - the hallmark of the henge. Twenty yards in front of me is the Heel Stone, over which the sun is due to appear shortly. A faint glimmer has already appeared on the horizon. As we wait, my mind drifts back to the last time I was here, ten years ago.

I can still remember the guide telling us that no one knows why those ancient people built Stonehenge, though there are plenty of theories. The experts do know that it was begun five thousand years ago, but its purpose remains a mystery…and now here I am…on the most important day of the year, huddled among the mass of pilgrims, druids, pagans, witches, and warlocks, with my back to the circle. Atop the Slaughter Stone, I have the perfect view of the Heel Stone, its stark figure cut against the sky behind it. They killed humans on this spot those "experts" used to think.

# Journey to Glastonbury

I look at my watch - three minutes to go. The druids increase their intense beat. Out of the corner of my eye, I notice a group of people that seem out of place. They are bald except for a single thin ponytail sticking out from the top of their shiny skulls, and their bodies are clad in bright orange robes as they chant. They form a circle around me.

One minute to go - the drumming is more intense, louder. The orange robed people are now shaking, their ponytails trying to keep up.

The yellow glow on the horizon increases - less than half a minute to go.

Over top the Heel Stone, a meteor streaks across the sky. My head snaps back...*he's here.*

A moment later the edge of the fiery orb reaches upward announcing the start of the summer solstice, and my feet grow warm. As the glimmer shines on the pale bluebell flowers that lie in the farmer's field next to the henge, the world dissolves away, and for a brief of moment, I am aware of Stonehenge's purpose.

# Part One – Sent Back in Time

# January 2nd, 2013

# The Orchid

*7:33 am, San Diego, California, USA*

Flailing, I am aware that I am no longer upright and my legs are not free. As I struggle for breath, a new challenge presents itself as I try to force my eyes open. They're glued shut from their own discharge. Through the murk, a single orchid catches my eye. It has two large purple and white flowers on long green stems. I remember this one because a friend of mine gave it to me as a housewarming gift and I had to figure out how to take care of it … and I did. I had placed it on the chest of drawers in my *old* bedroom, in the apartment I once knew before the horror began, and I kept it alive the whole time I lived in San Diego. I have not seen this delicate plant since I moved away in the fall of 2013 – almost ten years ago.

My chest is still heaving as I gasp for air. My legs are trapped beneath the blankets of my bed, my *old* bed. California sunshine sifts through the blinds on my left. I wipe the ooze from my eyes, and remain where I am. Only my eyes have motion, as they look from the orchid, to the window, at the open doorway leading into the living room, and finally at the textured ceiling. My eyeballs stop moving as I stare with unseeing eyes.

I kick back the bed covers. The color of the pale blue pajamas I'm wearing reminds me of the flowers I have just seen in the field next to Stonehenge.

# Journey to Glastonbury

The next hour is spent retching and vomiting in the bathroom until my stomach has voided its last meal. Still on my knees, I close the toilet seat and lay my head on it, my mouth tasting foul. I feel better, begin to relax, and my eyelids become heavy. In this twilight moment, the dark time of my life replays, as it has an infinite amount of times before.

My eyes open with a jolt of pain along the right side of my neck. As the pain subsides, my head clears allowing me to think. I sit back against the bathroom wall and whisper "This is *not* real. I am *not* in my old San Diego apartment. The year is *2023*, and *I am at Stonehenge.*"

Perhaps I fainted and hit my head on one of the Henge's little bluestones? Maybe I just need to … to what? If I am dreaming - or worse yet, delirious - how do I snap out of it?

I am suddenly aware of where I am, my back to the wall of my little bathroom, in my little apartment, back in San Diego – as if it's a decade ago.

With a wobble, I stand up, grabbing the marble countertop next to the toilet to steady myself. I look at my disheveled appearance in the mirror. "Whoa!" I say to myself. There is less white hair and more light brown atop my head. The crow's feet around my eyes are not as deep. The skin on my cheeks is tighter, my brow less furrowed. "I have hardly any wrinkles," I mutter. I turn my head to an angle – the bald spot on the crown of my head is gone.

I need to know the date.

I look around the apartment for a calendar upon the wall, or an electronic device that can give me the answer I seek, but I see none. As I move into the living room, the sun explodes through the open window. I close the drapes to dampen the brightness. Turning to my right I am face-to-face with a large television mounted on the wall. I turn it on and switch to a news network. The newscaster tells me that a missile fired from a drone has just killed eight members of a terror group. However, my eyes are not on the drone, they are on the date at the bottom of the television screen. It blares out like a silent scream.

Wednesday, January 2nd, *2013*

*"No, it can't be."*

I wait for the network to correct the date. I know they won't though, because deep down I know it is right. All I have to do is look around me.

Almost on their own, my legs begin to move, carrying me to the doorway just off the kitchen. Next to the door, a leather billfold stands atop a small telephone table. In it, I find everything I would expect in a ten-year-old wallet belonging to me. There is my California driver's license that is set to expire on my next birthday, a few hundred in cash, and several credit cards. One thing I cannot locate in my old home is a telephone of any kind. Likewise, the laptop that I know I had isn't here. At this time in my life, I usually left it at work.

Just like many people in the 21st century, I am lost without the internet. Next to the air I breathe, and the water that sustains me, I must be "connected". Even in this twilight moment, I feel compelled. I need that computer, if for nothing else just to research the strangeness that I am experiencing. Has this ever happened to anyone else at Stonehenge? Finding my closet full of my old clothing, I get dressed and begin the journey to fetch my laptop.

# Epiphany

*9:13 am, San Diego, California, USA*

The day is too warm for January. Even Californians aren't used to tropical weather at this time of year. Leaving by the front door of the apartment building, still feeling weak and nauseous, I can smell the green-gray water of the bay that is only three blocks away. I stop for a moment, surprised that I can sense the nearby sea, and then continue walking toward my old workplace while I look around me as if I've just been born. That sun that I woke up to causes me to squint.

Along the way, I pass rows of tall Mexican fan palms that line each side of the avenue. I also pass the shelters of the homeless, attracted to this part of the country by the mild climate. Foggy memories of when I used to live here pepper my walk. A few blocks to the left was my favorite pizza place, "Landini's"; to the right is where I used to buy my groceries. As I approach the building where my work is, I feel daunted. It's a thirty-story tower and I don't remember which floor my office is on. As I enter and look at the directory, the burly security guard in a dark suit says, "Can I help you?"

My mouth is dry. "I work here," I say without any confidence. He studies me and decides that whether I do or not, I am not a threat.

As I get off the elevator and prepare to enter through the doors of my eighth floor accounting firm a vaguely

18

remembered co-worker says "good morning". He looks at me strangely, and I imagine it must be because I'm looking at him the same way.

As I approach my workspace, I can see my old laptop. I let out a sigh of relief. Across from my area sits my old co-worker Ed, surrounded by photos of his wife and daughters. The girls had been ongoing topics of conversation for years, even long after I left this place, but today their exploits do not interest me. "Ed, what's the date?" I say, trying to sound normal.

"January 2nd," he replies with a smirk.

I chance a more specific question, "What year is it?"

He raises an eyebrow, looking up at me from his work in disbelief. "That must've been some New Year's Eve Party you went to! *2013*," he chuckles, amused.

Trying to look casual, I say "Happy New Year!" and extend my hand. He shakes it and says the same thing back.

I settle into my old chair and turn on my laptop computer. Just like the television in my apartment, it agrees with Ed's date. Just to the right of the keyboard is my smartphone. It's unusual that I forgot it at work, but I am thankful to the universe.

I click around on my computer for nearly an hour - reading old emails, researching phenomena associated with Stonehenge, and wrapping my head around the current events of the past. My confused eyes are locked on the screen when an instant message pops up.

"Hey. I just blew past two thousand fans on my page."
Next to the message is a little round image of a smiling
young man wearing sunglasses, the sea at his back. I feel a
surge of blood go to my brain as the message assaults me.
For a moment, I almost black out, but I emerge quickly. I
look over at Ed and the rest of my co-workers and take
comfort that no one noticed. If this was a normal time, I
might summon an ambulance fearing the onset of a stroke.
I remain frozen in my seat. "How long has it been since I
last saw him?" I almost whisper.

"2,610 now" the young man continues. He is referring to
his DJ fan page. Back in early 2013 social networking was
still new to me. Facebook, Twitter, and Instagram were
growing, and I was doing my best as an old-school guy to
keep up. I also had no idea what his DJ and music producer
career was all about...or where it would lead.

As my fingers slowly approach the keyboard, a rush of
adrenaline overcomes me sending my heart into overdrive,
pushing blood to my brain as I realize that I'm not "of this
time." In my mind, I have a *memory of his future* as I see
this young man on stage performing in front of thousands
of screaming fist pumping young fanatics. I stand up so
suddenly that my chair rolls to the back of my area. I'm
dizzy, so I sit back down again to avoid a tumble. My eyes
remain focused on my computer screen, but no further
messages strike at me. The moment overcomes my senses.

The young man's most successful songs play in my head as
I push the chair towards the computer. Only later do I
realize that some of these songs don't even exist yet. I lay

my fingers on the home keys of the keyboard and type. "Wow, Wyatt. You really blew past it." My delayed response doesn't seem to alarm him.

"One of my remixes went viral." Wyatt adds.

Phone in hand, I dash from my desk with a mumbled excuse that Ed pays no attention to and escape into an empty meeting room. My fingers tremble as I hold the telephone in front of me, almost afraid of its powers. At any moment, this gift may leave me as quickly as it arrived – this chance to change things. I begin to feel panic as I dial Wyatt's home number, amazed that I can still remember it after all this time. Then I hear an error message. He and his girlfriend Emily haven't moved into their apartment yet so the number isn't active. No wonder I don't have it in my contacts. However, his cell phone number is. Frantic, I press the connect button as my heart clenches with each ring. In one heart stopping moment there is a "click" on the other end of the line and a voice speaks.

"Hello?" It's him.

"Wyatt," I gasp, a sweat breaking across my forehead. "Wyatt."

"What's up dude? Is everything okay?" I cannot bring myself to answer, my eyes are swimming and I try to breathe. "Hello?" he repeats.

Feebly I say, "I just wanted to congratulate you on getting two thousand fans."

Sounding confused, he thanks me and nothing further is said other than good-bye. I can't bring myself to say, "Oh, by the way, I'm from ten years in the future."

I hang up as the full weight of this reality strikes me on the chin with a brash uppercut.

*This is real ...*

So is my fear as I realize what is coming.

There's nothing left but to go. Returning to my desk with haste, I say to Ed "I have an emergency." After packing up the laptop and placing my phone firmly in my pocket, I hurry out of the office.

As I bolt into the elevator, the events of the next two years race through my mind - the moment we discover the truth, our desperate actions, and how final it was.

A few hours later, I am boarding a 2pm flight.

# Flying into the Past

*2:15 pm, on the tarmac at San Diego International Airport*

"You stole my idea!" proclaims a man a few rows ahead of me on the airplane. The volume of his voice makes me wish I had earplugs. I can see that he holds a plastic cup in his left hand, while an empty Jack Daniels mini-bottle lies on his armrest.

We had just left the gate minutes ago, and are now taxiing towards the runway.

"Shut the hell up," says the red-faced man sitting next to him.

The two foes toss a few ugly words at each other, causing a pudgy male flight attendant to move down the aisle toward them. "If the pair of you continue, we'll return to the gate and you'll have to deal with security." The threat is enough to calm them down.

My eyelids close as I relax to the whirr of the jet engines, my thoughts drifting to the little boy with hazel eyes and messy hair that caused his own trouble so many years ago.

# Young Wyatt

He was about ten when he had his first run-in with the police. On this, the first of many occasions, it was for stealing a little girl's bike in his hometown of Keating Cross Road, a tiny rural community on heavily forested Vancouver Island. When the police brought the youth home to Margaret (his single mother) and detailed the crime, nodding to the pink tire jutting from the police cruiser's open trunk, she listened quietly before asking, "Can I take a look at the bike?"

Margaret considered the trunk of the cruiser for a brief moment before bursting into laughter that startled the officer, even as a crooked smile spread across her little boy's face.

"What's so funny?" the officer demanded. *Like mother like son*, he thought, believing he understood the source of the child's wayward behavior.

It took a minute for her to contain her humor "This is his sister's bike!"

Despite himself, the cop began to laugh as well.

The Keating Cross Road Police Department would get to know Wyatt over the years. Even as he caused trouble he endeared himself to them: mischievous enough to keep them on their toes but never causing any real harm ... and always the happiest little spark you ever met, even sitting in the back of a squad car.

# Journey to Glastonbury

*****

It was a few years after the bike incident that I had the first of my own experiences with Wyatt and the police. Margaret was in dire need of a vacation and asked if I might be willing to take care of the three children for a week in their home. I agreed without hesitation. Within an hour of her departure, I found Wyatt at the door with a police escort before I even realized he had left the house. He had been drinking. I directed my confusion to both the boy and the officer.

"Where does a thirteen year old get liquor?"

"He took it from a cabinet on his way out." The officer gave Wyatt a light tap on the back of his head making his shoulder length dark brown hair shimmer in the sunlight. "Wanted to show off for a few friends, I'm guessing."

Trying not to laugh at Wyatt's dazed expression, I promised to keep a close eye on him and he was released into my custody. I exercised my temporary authority by grounding him for a week and watched him become the perfect teen. He did chores around the house, came home right after school, did his homework, and never once asked to hang out with his friends. After five days of his best behavior, I relented on the punishment and released him back into society.

When the doorbell rang that same evening, I took a deep breath and braced myself. The same officer was there, uniform rumpled, holding Wyatt by the arm. Society wasn't quite ready.

"Brawl," he said without any greeting, irritation etched on his face. Wyatt had a large shiner on his left eye. "Thought he could fight a full grown man. Get outta my sight kid." Wyatt disappeared into the house without meeting my eyes and when the officer was sure he was gone, his face took on another look. He lowered his voice and with a Cheshire cat's smile said, "You should see the other guy. That kid can pack a punch."

\*\*\*\*\*

As he turned into a gangly fifteen-year-old things didn't improve much. At his high school, he transformed the hallways into full-blown parties, much to the admiration of his fellow students, and the chagrin of those in charge. On his younger sister's first day of high school, sitting in her first class, she glanced up from her notebook to see her brother fly down the hall piloting a shopping cart with two other students pushing. Wyatt was suspended… again.

Like most teenagers, he survived this chaotic period relatively unscathed. However, unlike most troublemaking teens, he transformed like a rough piece of coal into something altogether different. As he turned sixteen, every scrap of his childhood personality was harnessed and served to propel him into the change. It was during that year that he and his family left their small town of Keating Cross Road for the nearby city of Victoria, and it was there that he discovered his talent for music production.

This was also when he met Emily.

# Nature's Disgust

*6:36 pm, Victoria International Airport, Canada*

By the time I step off the airplane I've already decided that I'm not going to blurt out "Hey, guess what…I'm from the future!" …to anybody. I need to be slow, subtle and careful. I need to be credible if I am to change things.

"Give me anything," I say to the woman behind the rental car counter. After ten minutes that seem like ten hours, she hands me a set of car keys. I'm anxious to get to Margaret's house on Chestnut Street where I hope to find Wyatt. At that moment, it occurs to me that in my haste I forgot to tell anyone I was coming.

Half an hour later, I park under an overhang of barren oak. The wet January ground nearly pitches me into a carpet of decomposing leaves. Christmas lights flash through my peripheral vision. There is a slight drizzle coming from the smothering dark gray sky overhead… *like nature spitting its disgust that I would try to alter a future that it had already decided.*

# I Meet Wyatt

*7:39 pm, Victoria, British Columbia, Canada*

I look up and down the street, and then walk briskly to the door. After ringing the bell twice, a wide-eyed Margaret answers. She can read the disappointment on my face as I say, "Is Wyatt here?" Only later do I realize that I didn't even say hello to her.

Standing in the dim light I wait for Wyatt to come to the door, and it suddenly feels a lot colder out here than it really is. The light rain that is falling seeps down my forehead. A million thoughts float through my mind - how many years has it been since I last saw him? I used to spend all my Christmases here at this time of my life, so Wyatt just saw me a few days ago, but for me, coming from 2023, it's been years.

I've been standing out here an eternity, and if I hadn't heard Margaret yell to Wyatt that he was wanted at the door, and his answer back, I might've thought I'd been forgotten. Am I really going to see him? This cannot be happening.

I think about those ten years, in that life leading up to Stonehenge… the time between now and then, and everything that has or will happen. I do not want to repeat them - the emptiness that followed - and suddenly, breaking through my thoughts…

"What are you doing here? I thought you were in San Diego?" Wyatt says.

I cannot reply because my senses are overloaded. I don't feel the cold anymore, or the moisture running down my left cheek. He says something else, but I can't hear. The world is spinning as I put my hand on the dark green doorframe to keep from falling. I begin to register him - tall, gangly, light brown hair, big soft eyes. This is not how I remember him, yet I know that it really is Wyatt.

"Dude, do we need to call an ambulance?" His smile has given way to a frown.

Finally, I am able to talk. "No. I'm okay." I take my hand off the doorframe and hold myself up. I can feel my heartbeat pulsing and pounding, like I just ran a mile. He chuckles in relief and invites me in, and I enter as if I am walking into a dream... but I know this is not a dream, this is real. Once again I fear a return to Stonehenge in 2023. *I want to stay here. I want this second chance.* "I flew back to take care of some unfinished business," I continue as my heartbeat and ability to converse return to normal. At that moment, a long forgotten memory of him moving into a new home at this time of his life pokes into my consciousness. "So ... I bet you're excited about your first apartment with Emily?" I am proud that I can remember this old detail.

"Em and I are so stoked!" His eyes glow with enthusiasm. "Em" is his long-time girlfriend, Emily.

A vague recollection from long ago pops into my head: Wyatt showing me the outside of their new place when I was here for the holidays. "We're moving our stuff in the Friday after next." He adds.

I continue to stall. I don't want to leave. "Aside from your fan base topping 2,000, what's new in the music business?"

Enthusiasm floods through Wyatt. "I'm working on this trippy new tune. I'll play it for you next time you come over. I'm also doing a lot of gigs this month."

"That's great, Wyatt. Do you think I can come to one of them?"

"Sure," he says, but I know that when the time comes he'll tell me he needs to focus and my presence "cramps his style". By this time, I'd only ever seen him perform once.

It is as a DJ and music producer that Wyatt will achieve success. He's already grown popular enough to sign with Skid Row Records, even though he's only twenty years old. By this coming summer the promotions of his record company will see his music begin to chart amidst rave reviews from international music magazines. Primetime commercials will begin utilizing his productions, and some of the world's most famous DJ's and music producers will take note of his talent. However, he does not know any of this yet, but I do… I have lived it already.

*****

Wyatt's music career began shortly after his sixteenth birthday when a friend invited him to attend an electronic music festival. It was a summertime event where some of the top DJ's in the world would perform, artists like Skrillex, Jean-Paul, and Diplo. With a love of music already engrained in him, Wyatt witnessed a spectacle that would change his life - the live performances required musical talent, energy, a love of dancing, exuberance, and uninhibited performance. In that moment he realized that his blend of gifts made him uniquely qualified. On that day, his DJ alter ego "Lewd Behavior" was born.

When it comes to Wyatt's music career, I identify with what it must have felt like to be an old man in the 1950's encountering the new phenomenon of "rock 'n' roll." Wyatt's music is confusing, loud, and unlike anything I'd heard before. I remember that it made me realize my own age - my first experience on the wrong end of the generation gap.

*****

As we move out onto the front stoop the cold sets in and we're both starting to shiver. As much as I loathe leaving, I can't stand at the door forever, and he only has a dark blue sweater for warmth. "It's getting late Wyatt. I'm going to try and get a room at the Empress. I'll call you tomorrow."

# City of Gardens, Island of Rain Forests

*8:45 pm, Victoria, British Columbia, Canada*

The twenty-minute drive passes slowly at first. Despite the absence of traffic, I can't help but take my time in the right lane, relishing the mystery and beauty that is Victoria. With access to the island upon which it sits only available by ferry or airplane, the population has stayed small and the natural beauty has gone largely untouched. This is a place of endless gardens, flowerpots hanging from the streetlamps, and mile high trees. The evergreen rainforests are lush with age-old secrets, green and vibrant with life even now in the dead of winter. The sun has long since vanished and my headlights reflect off the fresh rain coating the roads. The oncoming lights shimmer and each time they pass, I find myself caught in the tension that they will send me away, back to the Stonehenge of 2023. The Douglas firs begin to feel as though they are looming overhead, closing in behind me as soon as I pass them and inching closer. I press down on the gas, anxious to leave them far behind.

I can still feel the journey and the day's travel taking its toll on my mind and body as I check into the Empress Hotel, an iconic Edwardian chateau built in the heart of the city over a hundred years ago. Thankfully, the end of the holidays has made for plenty of vacancies and in no time at all I'm laying on the king-size bed in my fourth floor room. I'm sure this is the hotel I stayed at when I visited over the

Christmas break. For all I know, I was in this very room just a few days ago.

The ivy covered Empress is across the street from the ocean, and from my open window I can hear waves crashing in the distance. The view is split between the jewel box lights of downtown and the vast darkness of the sea. Even plunged into the depths of winter night, I know the buildings of the city's skyline like the back of my hand. I strain my eyes, working my way from the illuminated outline of the baroque styled Parliament building to the quiet rush of downtown to where I know the little French restaurant Camille's is tucked away, couples hunched nearly forehead-to-forehead over their candlelit dinner tables. I can feel an ache form in my chest, more potent than all of the day's exhaustions combined. Camille's - where sometimes love flourishes, and sometimes where it ends. I picture Wyatt and Emily there.

# Emily

Emily is calm and collected, always in control of her emotions, and you feel like you don't know a lot about her. Even under extreme duress or times of tragedy, Wyatt's girlfriend is remarkably composed.

The two are opposites. While Wyatt's emotions are always on display, there is a shell around Emily that only he can pierce. Even after knowing her for many years, and spending countless hours with her, this shell persists.

Her hair is a cross between copper and mahogany, her complexion fair with a dash of freckles thrown in. She's a petite young lady, with delicate features and almond shaped green eyes.

From her actions, I know that Emily likes to care for things. Her many plants thrive, as does her black cat and her little black bunny. She loves "collectibles," objets d'art that are not quite old enough to be called antique. The apartment that her and Wyatt are about to move into is itself heirloom quality, built in the 1920's, and she will immediately love it and consider it "home", something she would not have felt had it been a contemporary place.

Currently, Emily works two jobs, one involving occasional night work, and the other in a clothing store at the mall. When she works the midnight shift, Wyatt is always there to drive her home, no matter what time it is or what he's doing the next day.

Emily's unspoken dream is to one day have a family with
Wyatt. She yearns for the stable, traditional household that
neither she nor he ever had. Consequently she supports
Wyatt's musical ambitions, while at the same time
motivating him to continue his education and gain a skill
that could one day support a family. In her mind's eye she
can see her and Wyatt celebrating their golden years
surrounded by the love of their children and their children's
children. Oh … and lots of houseplants, bunnies, cats and
dogs … and maybe even a horse like the one she has over
at her mom's acreage.

Wyatt is her soul mate and they *will* grow old together. Of
that she is certain.

# Love Blossoms

As Emily tells it the two met at a house party - four years before this new time that I'm in. "Who's this weirdo who keeps asking me for a hug?" she thought. Unable to get a hug, Wyatt persisted in asking for her phone number. Again and again, she resisted, but the gangly teenager with a wide smile and too much enthusiasm wore her down. They went on several dates without any contact between them, aside from a polite embrace at the end of each and a kiss on the cheek. A few weeks later, on New Year's Eve, they kissed. They have been inseparable ever since.

Early in their relationship they discovered a common interest that bonded them: electronic dance music. She loved to dance and in Wyatt she found her equal. The two met just as his own music career was beginning, and she would be his biggest fan and supporter.

By Wyatt's nineteenth birthday, he and Emily had been dating for over three years. This is when Wyatt's "mid-life" crisis kicked in. He figured that it was time to try out the *other* life… that of a single guy. What I witnessed was a young man who was ready to have fun on a moment's notice, but whose high-paced life was not sustainable. Thankfully, the high-octane lifestyle did not last long because he soon figured out it lacked a girl he couldn't be without. That's also when I realized that without Emily, Wyatt is like an un-tethered kite floating high up in the clouds.

In the new reality that I'm in, ten years in the past, Wyatt is now twenty having successfully emerged from that mid-life crisis with Emily still by his side.

# Part Two – Changing the Future

# The Message

*January 3, 2013, Victoria, British Columbia, Canada*

*9:09 am*

*I dream ...*

*"You need to go to Seattle," Wyatt's grandfather says.*

I am suddenly awake, remembering the glint of his eyes. I have not heard his voice in years. A wave of fear causes me to check the date on my phone.

*January third, 2013.* I exhale deeply, realizing only then that I had been holding my breath.

The room is freezing. I get up to close the window of my suite at the hotel, and Victoria is still spread out in front of me as I pull open the curtains, grateful to be blinded by the morning light. I do my best to shake myself out of the dream, setting the coffeepot to brew and turning on the clock radio. A few minutes later, a song begins to play on the local radio station that causes my hand to slip as I shave, a small trail of blood working its way through the shaving foam. It's one of Wyatt's remixes.

As I listen to the music, and wipe away the trickle of blood, it dawns on me that the old man is right - we do need to make the short trip across the water to Seattle. I can feel my blood pulsing in time with the 160 beats per minute of Wyatt's production, keenly aware of every passing moment. I think of the genetic problem behind our misery, and suddenly feel like time is a countdown. If I do not alter the future, suffering and grief lay ahead. I search the internet on my laptop, find a phone number, and make a call. We'll be there in a week.

.

# The Dinner

*January 3, 2013, Victoria, British Columbia, Canada*

*6:07 pm*

I am at the restaurant Wyatt suggested for our dinner tonight. No one else is here yet.

I strain my eyes looking for the ocean, the light from the restaurant the only thing that reveals the vast murkiness only inches away. The skies are dark and when water flecks the glass, it's impossible to tell if it is rain or ocean spray. Wyatt's sister, Taylor, arrives shortly after me, and she stands out despite being hardly taller than the ficus trees that stand next to the entrance. I'm somewhat startled to see that her hair is bright green again, having become used to her natural color in the years ahead.

"I'm going to be rich!" She sings by way of greeting. "I got that job!"

"Congratulations!" I say, with no recollection of the job she is referring to.

"Thanks. It pays so much better, and Camille's is such a beautiful restaurant…and there are always great tips."

*She looks so young*, I think to myself. "I'm so happy for you, Taylor." I remember when she quit Camille's to focus on school. "You look amazing, by the way. That outfit looks like it came straight out of Europe." I had been in

Paris two days prior to my trip to Stonehenge, and she would have fit right in.

"Speaking of outfits," she calls out, "check out the hippie!" Although he rolls his eyes at his sister's teasing, Anthony can't suppress his smile.

"Yeah, nice to see you too, Taylor," he replies before turning to me, pale blue eyes warm. "I didn't expect to see you back so soon."

If only he knew how long I've really been gone. "Yup. I couldn't stay away." I reply as I stand to shake his hand and laugh nervously. He stands a few inches taller than me, lanky underneath his tie-dyed sweatshirt. Just then, a burst of laughter at the door announces Wyatt's arrival, Emily and Margaret in tow.

A short while later a waiter takes our orders.

"I'll have the miso salmon, please," Emily is the last to order, and I stare at her in surprise.

"Salmon?" I ask, as my eyes narrow. "What happened to being vegan?" The family looks at me, confused.

"I'm not vegan," Emily speaks awkwardly to me as well as the waiter. "I may be vegan someday, I don't know..." she trails off. I sit with my foot in my mouth.

"Sorry, sorry," I cough, "I must have forgotten." The last word elicits a look of confusion from the group. *Forgot what?* I could kick myself. She'll be a vegan sometime in the future, but that decision is still a few years off.

# Dream a Little Dream

*January 3, 2013– still at the restaurant*

*6:41 pm*

It almost doesn't matter what you say, the next thing that comes out of anybody's mouth is going to send our table into rolling-on-the-floor laughter. The couple eating dinner at the table next to us is trying to be romantic, and I overhear them telling each other where they work and what they like to do in their spare time. *This is their first date*, I think to myself. As the guy tries to impress the young lady, he finds himself interrupted by the chortle of our table. They both look at us with disdain.

"So I'm cruising the web using this app called 'StumbleUpon', you know the one," says Wyatt, "It takes you to cool websites. Completely random. And it takes me to a site showing virtual-reality goggles… very cool stuff." Wyatt says.

"You'd look awesome in a pair of those," says Emily.

Wyatt nods, amidst the giggles. "After then it takes me to this listing of people who will break into places to pull off insurance scams. You know, like climb into hi-rise apartments, get past security systems. They're called cat burglars …."

"Yeah. And the worst part is… they don't even steal cats." Em interjects.

Everyone chuckles, but Wyatt gives her a confused look. It lasts about a half a second, until he sees her face and coy grin. His own face beams as he realizes that she is joking.

"The next place that StumbleUpon takes me is a website called 'How to get tickets to Glastonbury Festival'."

"What's that?" says Margaret.

"It's sort of like Coachella," interjects Taylor, referring to the massive California music festival, "except bigger and more bizarre."

The girl from the first date couple chimes in, now looking interested instead of irritated. "I want to go Glasto so bad!" Now their table is joining in on our humor.

Anthony, who's sort of like a walking encyclopedia, says, "Glastonbury is a music and art festival every summer in the south of England. I heard they had a million and a half requests for the tickets, sold out in half an hour – two hundred thousand tickets in half an hour! And you can't even get them from a scalper, because they are tied to your photo ID. The Rolling Stones are one of the headliners this year."

"I love the Stones!" says Margaret, chuckling.

"Can I go with you?" says the now smiling girl at the next table to Wyatt. A hurt look flashes on her date's face, and I'm briefly surprised that Emily doesn't feel threatened by the flirting. Then I remember, from the coming years, how devoted they are to one another. This girl, though attractive, has about as much chance of getting Wyatt interested as she has of getting a ticket to Glastonbury.

Suddenly, time slows down and a surreal hush overcomes the restaurant. Wyatt, his face now serious, breaks the silence by saying "Maybe one day, I'll be popular enough to play at Glasto. That's my dream, I guess"

He wears a far-away look on his face. I know where he is. In his mind, Wyatt is on stage performing in front of thousands of crazed fans, rain pouring from the sky, mud enveloping the feet of those fanatics.

# Something to Tell

*January 5, 2013, Victoria, British Columbia, Canada*

*7:01 am*

I have been in Victoria for three nights, insomnia a close friend of mine. It's still pitch black outside and once again, I'm wide-awake. I've had maybe three hours. Tossing and turning is all I can do. I'm anxious to call Wyatt, but it's way too early, especially on a Saturday. As the clock continues to countdown, the January sun frustrates me with its tardiness. Finally, at eight in the morning, I call.

"Hello?" Wyatt's voice is groggy.

"Good morning Wyatt. How are you?"

"Um… I'm good, I guess… sleepy. Is something wrong?"

"No, I'm fine. I was just wondering if you can meet me here at the hotel this afternoon?"

"What? You mean like 'high tea at the Empress'?" he chuckles.

Afternoon Tea at the famous Empress Hotel is what the tourists do. "No, I was thinking we could just grab a coffee and go for a walk. I have something I want to talk to you about."

# DNA

*January 5, 2013*

*12:36 pm*

As I fidget in one of the hotel's wingtip chairs, I see Wyatt through the windows, handing the keys of his Toyota to the valet. He keeps it immaculate, and I can remember the hours of work he put in just to give it the look of dual exhaust pipes.

As he enters, the geometric patterns of the tile floor create the illusion of a walkway extending from the door to me. I can clearly see the graphics on the front of his sweatshirt, proud capital letters that say "Property of Skid Row Records".

"Dude, I charged the valet to your room."

"That's fine." I strain for a smile. "They serve coffee just down that hall."

"Let's take it to go, maybe see a little more of this awesome place. I'm thinking a walk on the water front would be nice," says Wyatt.

"Sounds like a plan," I smile back.

The sun breaks through for a moment, causing the roads to shine wetly in a light fog. The bright orb in the sky feels like an omen and I bask in it for a moment. The sunlight reflects off the storefronts, while the glass panes of the

Victorian street lamps glow despite the time of day. A few minutes later the clouds move in again to cast a gray pall over the city.

Our coffee steams on the short walk to the ocean, and we are still laughing at the evil eye we got from the front desk worker when he saw us taking the white ceramic mugs out of the lobby.

The shoreline is dotted with quaint old buildings, elegant and stalwart in the face of the ocean mist each morning. Vines creep up the sides of some, while pinprick lights cover the façades of others and twinkle warmly off the water. There are a few sailboats out, their white sails mingling with the sea gulls, and the tide laps at the shore like the placid water of a lake.

"Let's sit down for a moment." I gesture to one of the benches on the esplanade and the smile leaves Wyatt's face for a moment as he realizes I'm about to tell him something important.

"Okay," he says.

More than once, I've imagined how this would go had Wyatt woken up three days ago in my position… ten years in the past. I can almost hear him "I'm so stoked. I've seen the future and it's awesome!"

He and I are very different. I look into his eyes. "I want you to take a trip with me to Seattle next week."

A floatplane chooses this moment to make its landing on the inky harbor, taking advantage of the calm water, and the noise of the propeller stops Wyatt from replying for several seconds. He maintains eye contact until the sun suddenly breaks through the cloud and illuminates his face, forcing him to look away so I can no longer gauge his expression."Why? What's up?" he pauses for a moment, and when I am slow to answer he continues, "I have projects for school and classes, and I've been hired by this South African band to do some remixes on their hit singles. They're paying me a lot of money... and, Em and I are moving into our new place, like, soon. I'm really, really busy."

"Wyatt, I wouldn't ask you if it wasn't important. We can take your car and I'll cover gas, food, everything. We'll make it fun. You can also work onboard the ferry."

Wyatt doesn't bite, and the smile leaves his face "You've been acting strange since you got back to town. You drag me over here ... why don't you just tell me what this is all about?"

I almost tell him - *hey, I was just in 2023 a few days ago and know a few things about the future. Just do what I tell you and everything will work out...hopefully*"

I remain mute, causing his patience to crack, "Just freaking tell me!"

Up until this point, I didn't know how to. Then, like a bolt of lightning, inspiration strikes. "I think you may have a genetic problem."

His brow furrows and a crease appears on his forehead as he studies me, trying to figure out if this is another one of my inappropriate jokes, but I plunge forward. "It's hard to explain. It has to do with a gene. I'm no expert, but scans we can buy in Seattle will tell us if there's anything going on."

"What? Shouldn't Taylor and Anthony go too?"

"Eventually. But they're low risk."

There is a pause between us before Wyatt speaks again. "So I'm high risk? What makes you think that?"

Still riding a wave of inspiration, I say, "Because I have it, and you're a tall male in the high risk age category." Although I made this stuff up just now, it may be true. I already know Wyatt has a problem, and since it's genetic it has to have come from either his mother (Margaret) or myself.

# Broken

The love between Margaret and I had morphed into something destructive, a relationship based on disdain and cruelty. I knew that I had destroyed my family every bit as much as Margaret and in my anguish, I left. My heart was broken and the further I traveled the more I was able to escape the gravitational pull of the people I loved. My family was the center of my life and it had disintegrated. When the job in Hong Kong opened, I didn't think twice. To this day, the decision haunts me. My children would suffer and I knew it, but I could no longer face my estranged wife or the atmosphere we had made. It was the easy way out. I sent every cent of my money to support my children, regularly, and forced myself to think that this could make up for the lack of a father.

Even when the job in Hong Kong had ended I drifted, like a rowboat in the middle of the sea without oars. I worked in Germany, France, and Washington DC before the tides brought me to California—each new assignment bringing me closer to them, even as I spent my life away from my children. I visited occasionally, brought gifts from my exotic homes, and month-after-month I sent back all the money I had, doing everything I could not to acknowledge that what they really needed was me.

Time is a remedy, and each time I returned to my kids, the gravity pulled me in, longer and closer, until I was finally spending real time with them. By then, I had been away for nearly five years, and the damage had been done. When I did see them, they were unruly, disobedient, and always iron-willed. As much as I wanted to be with them again, I was overwhelmed by the consequences of my absence.

Several weekends passed visiting my children, each destroyed by my futile attempts at discipline. When I realized that I dreaded the next weekend of fighting with them alone, I resorted to my last idea. I took them to their grandparent's house.

# Rebuilding

My parents raised me in the far North, where the cold skies of winter were clear and illuminated nightly by the dance of the Northern lights. Even the sun was an enemy in the cold, fragmenting dangerously off of snowdrifts and forcing sunglasses amidst temperatures as low as negative thirty degrees. But the cold hardened me and shaped me, I snatched at warmer days and threw myself into skating or building forts in the snow until I had only white Christmas lights for illumination. My home had been magical for me and I could only hope it would work its magic on my children.

Within moments of arriving, after rapid hellos, all three of them vanished into the yard screaming, visible only by the telltale bobbing of their tricolored hats from above the snowdrifts. I could hardly bring myself to say hello to my own parents. It wasn't until later that evening when several cups of cocoa had eased the children's misbehavior and my own misery that their grandfather saw fit to intervene, giving me one of the last and most important pieces of advice that he would ever give me.

"Don't try to be their father right now. They have a parent, and it isn't you, not anymore and not from half a world away. All they need from you is love. Maybe in time things will be different."

Although I grieved what I had lost, I leaned on his advice as a crutch in my following visits. I spent time taking the kids to museums, watching old classic movies, or observing float planes land in the bay—and when all else failed, we made the drive to grandma and grandpa's house for secret recipe pancakes, snow days, and an abundance of hot chocolate. Slowly but surely, I reentered the lives of Anthony, Taylor and Wyatt. Out of the ashes of our divorce, Margaret and I found our common ground once again in our children and we were able to exist in each other's lives as friends. A rarity for divorced adults, but a privilege. We were able to be a family again. Without illusion of reconciliation, even amongst the children, we reached happiness together in one another's company. Laughter always flowed from our gatherings. Although we were no longer a normal nuclear family, we had found our way back together. I was visiting as often as work would allow, every holiday and occasional long weekends. The urge to travel had left me, and all I wanted was to be a part of my children's lives. I drove Taylor to gymnastics, listened to Wyatt and Anthony make music, and attended parent teacher conferences. I felt much as though life had offered me a new purpose that I never fully understood until I had nearly lost it. I was able to be a father again.

I worked hard to be present in their lives, to use their grandfather's wisdom to earn the relationships of my children once again. However, it was Wyatt, more than anyone, who really brought me back in. He led the family, as he so often did, welcoming me each time I returned. In the beginning from Hong Kong, to the present from California. Despite my failings, he had wanted a relationship with me as much as I wanted one with him. He had determinedly Skyped me at least twice a week, often calling as a joke even when I was visiting Victoria. The day he told me that I had been his motivation to enter business school was a turning point for both of us. From that point, we talked about business as much as family and music. He asked for my advice and used it in school as well as in the lives of the people he cared for. He dedicated himself to working for experience, and used his new knowledge to bolster the success of his mother's flower shop. For the first time in his life he was exactly the student any teacher could hope for. He blossomed under the increased challenges of the college level and brought success to the people he loved just as he found it in his own life.

# Return from Seattle

*January 10, 2013, aboard the MV Coastal Celebration*

*3:52 pm*

It's the following Thursday afternoon, and after getting the scans we need in Seattle, Wyatt and I are onboard a huge ferry on our way back to his island home of Victoria.

The restaurant on the upper deck features floor to ceiling windows all around and through them, the Pacific Ocean sparkles cerulean and various islands dot the horizon, forested in deep green. Sometimes you can see a pod of killer whales hunting in our wake, the sight of which spurs hundreds of passengers to the same side and causes the ship to list. Today though, the whales don't make themselves seen. However, the sky is filled with the vivid white wings of gulls that circle us, hoping for scraps, and occasionally I think I see seals making their way up onto the island shore.

Wyatt returns from the buffet with a heaping plate and the sun catches his eyes as he sits down. They're a deep hazel-green with a copper ring around the pupil, as though the bristles and trunks of the cedar trees of his homeland became a deep enough part of him to shine out on their own.

"What?" He looks up from his plate, noticing that I've been looking at him for a moment too long.

"Nothing," I say hastily. I reach for the newspaper in front of me as distraction, but I'm restless and it can't hold my attention for long.

"So, are you still going to help us move into our new place tomorrow?" Wyatt asks.

"Of course," I reply. Then I change the subject. "How have things been going with Skid Row?"

"Awesome!" he smiles. "They're huge in the dance scene." I took my jacket off, but he's still wearing the sweatshirt they sent him.

"Nice." I struggle to keep my tone fully casual. "Have they done anything for you since you signed?" He had reminded me on the trip down to Seattle that the contract with them was just a few weeks old.

Wyatt stops eating for a moment and takes a sip of juice. "They've gotten me a few remixing gigs so far, like that South African group I told you about. I'm hoping that soon they'll have gigs for me in other cities too, and music production jobs. Stuff like that. Also, I'm not supposed to mention anything because it's all still in the works," he leans towards me conspiratorially, "but they might set me up with a European tour!"

I nearly choke on the air. I know that one of his dreams is going to come true, but it may not be the right one.

# Moving Day

*January 11, 2013, Victoria, British Columbia, Canada*

*7:11: am*

When I wake up the next morning, my chest is tight, constricting with the weight of today. January eleventh, the day Wyatt and Emily move in and begin their lives together. Two years from now this day will take on a different meaning. There will be nothing said or done to mark it, and I remind myself that it is a blessing and not a curse that no one around me understands what I feel. The tightness in my chest will go unmentioned.

On my way to their new place I stop for coffees—two with cream, one with soymilk. As I drive I remember that Emily still hasn't transitioned to veganism; the soy will have to be mine. From the outside, the apartment looks exactly as I remember, and the curb is already strewn with their sofa and end tables, slightly less aged than the last time I saw them.

"Good Morning!" Wyatt's voice echoes from the inside of a moving van and he emerges with his face hidden behind a shaky stack of boxes.

"I brought coffee!" I say, holding up the tray.

"Oh, yes," he groans his appreciation as I hand him a medium sized paper cup with steam coming from a little hole in the plastic top. "Emily's just gone inside to check things out. Peggy's here, too."

As if on cue, Emily's mother comes around the corner of the van.

"Nice to see you again." Peggy waves, and for a moment I'm confused not to be wrapped in a characteristic hug. I remember suddenly that up to this point, we'd only briefly met, before the perils of life had brought us as close as any family.

"Peggy, great to see you. I have a soy coffee here, if that's your sort of thing."

"Lovely," she raises her eyebrows, "I've been off the dairy train for years." I, of course, already know this. In my imagination, I can see her decked out in the flowery robes of the seventies.

I look longingly at the final steaming cup in the tray. "I brought you a coffee, Emily," I say as I walk over to her. She stops measuring the doorway and with a soft smile says, "I need one. Thank you."

"Okay. Keep in mind that this is a pretty old building. So, no elevator." Wyatt points to the narrow staircase leading up to their door. I shiver at the sight, remembering the difficulty he had getting up and down those stairs back in the life that I remember. "Let's just go for it, kick things off with the couch."

Their new place is a unit in a converted 1930's home, each carefully shaped window a testament to the character that modern construction fails to match. The structure, once home to a single family, has since been converted into four apartments, and Emily and Wyatt's is one of two on the upper floor. Maneuvering the sofa up the old stairs is quite a production. With Emily's direction and our collective muscle, we tip the sofa onto its end in order to climb the stairs, and back down to fit through the door. Once it's been set down, Wyatt asks me through heavy breathing, "So, what do you think of the place?"

I feign unfamiliarity with the apartment, walking slowly through the living room. "It's beautiful," I reply, and my enthusiasm is genuine. The room is filled with soft light that filters through the clouds and then the veranda windows and my shoes are dappled with rose and orange. As I look up from them, I notice the ornate stained glass window sitting over the door, sending its colors across the bare carpet... and my footwear.

"That's original glass," Peggy tells me after setting a box down. "You should have heard Emily the day they found this place. I think she loves it almost as much as she loves Wyatt. First-sight basis, you know. Auras attract." Emily, her own box in hand, blushes.

"Yes," Wyatt agrees. "I've got stiff competition. Pops, do you want to see the other balcony? It's over here, off the kitchen. Technically, it's just part of the roof, so you have to climb through the window, but I think it counts." He spends the next several minutes showing me the rest of the apartment before reaching the conclusion that if we want to sit down, we'll have to move in the rest of the furniture. Soon afterwards all the heavy lifting is over, leaving stacks of boxes on the remaining available floor space of their six hundred square foot home.

"You girls can settle in," Wyatt suggests, "My dad and I are picking up pizza."

"Mom, will a little cheese be okay?" Emily asks.

"Well, I suppose it is a special occasion," she concedes, and smacks Wyatt's outstretched hand in a high five. "We'll be unpacking boxes."

Emily glances over from the windowsill, where she's carefully set several potted plants. A teal ceramic pot, overflowing with tendrils of ivy, leans against the frame. It will eventually grow up the wall and around the window, flourishing in the light. Delicate flowers blossom in a variety of antique teacups and a small cactus bristles from its perch in a soil-filled terrarium. "Could you pick up Bunny and Kitty too?" she says to Wyatt while continuing to arrange the plant life.

# A Toast

*January 11, 2013, Victoria, British Columbia, Canada*

*4:28: pm*

It is late afternoon when we return, burdened with pizzas, a six pack of Wyatt's Blue Buck ale, and two furry black creatures. In the hour we've been gone, the apartment has already begun to transform. Lamps warm the room with light; a crimson Indian rug is unrolled on the living room floor, and soft strains of music drift from Emily's turntable, set up on top of the speaker system in the corner. Peggy dangles from a stepladder where she is hanging heavy lace curtains from the veranda window, nails sticking out from her pursed lips. When we enter, Emily straightens up from next to the door where she's placed an antique metal milk pail.

"For umbrellas," she explains to Wyatt, a serene smile on her face. "I found it at the antique store in Cook Street Village last weekend. Mom brought it over in her truck."

"You're the dopest," Wyatt exclaims, "However, I brought pizza and Dad brought beer, so we might be close to even." He leans over the animal carrier in his arms and gives Emily a kiss on the forehead. "Is it safe to release Bunny?"

Although the air is chilling rapidly as the sun sets, we eat our pizza on the veranda. The weather matters little to us because we are celebrating. Wyatt and I share a large Hawaiian, Emily and Peggy work through a vegetarian.

Kitty is sitting next to us scanning the yard below, ready to scurry back into the house at the first threat. If she does, she will be chased back out by the furry long eared boss hopping through the living room.

It suddenly occurs to me that not a word has been mentioned about our trip to Seattle the day before, nor the genetic problem, and for this I am grateful.

"Cheers," Wyatt says, raising his beer.

"Cheers," the rest of us reply, and the air is punctuated with the icy sound of clinking glass.

"To the rest of our lives," Wyatt pulls Emily in towards his chest, his arm around her shoulder. For a rare moment, I can read Emily well. She is blissful. Just as quickly, though, the moment passes and her face is a mystery again. Suddenly, the date hits me squarely in the chest - *to the rest of their lives.*

# Thirty Days *after*

*February 1, 2013, Victoria, British Columbia, Canada*

Dr. Markham was Wyatt's doctor the last time we experienced this, in the timeline that only I remember, the one before Stonehenge sent me back to relive this all over again. I am not surprised when I hear her voice – sort of like a person who was born and raised in England, but with a hint of a Dutch accent mixed in. Canada is a land of immigrants, and she is an example, having lived most of her life down in South Africa.

"You can see it right here." She shows us a scan on a computer screen and we all feign that we see something, but we don't. To our untrained eye, there is nothing, just pictures that we're told are of Wyatt's hip. I look around the overcrowded room of her office, in a building that was once a house located just a few blocks from the hospital. The walls are light brown wood paneling, the type that was popular back in the 70's. Either the doctor isn't doing well financially, or she just doesn't want to spend money to update the place. Given that she's a specialist, I'm sure it's the latter. Wyatt sits in a chair next to Emily, his right hand on her left. Margaret is there too, concern etched on her face.

The doctor had received Wyatt's scans and reports from the medical imaging place we went to in Seattle a few weeks ago. "Don't be alarmed, but this little blemish on the screen is a tumor." I look around at my family members, and I can see the shine of fear in their eyes. I've been through this before, so the discovery is no surprise to me. I already know it's there, and I know what it is.

The room is quiet until Emily, who has returned to her stoic self asks, "What does this mean?"

"It looks like cancer … bone cancer." The oncologist replies.

A glassy stare appears on Margaret's face as Wyatt says, "What the hell?" His hand grips Emily's, but she shows no signs of pulling away. The initial hint of anger in his voice gives way to an uncertain laugh "I feel great. I've never felt better than I do now. Geez, I'm only twenty."

"I know how old you are." His doctor replies with a hint of irritation. "All I can tell you is that this looks like early stage cancer. I have no idea what prompted you to get these scans. It'll be months before you feel this; months before you should even know it's inside of you. But there it is, and we need to get a biopsy, so I'm referring you to an oncology surgeon."

# Flashback

Still in Doctor Markham's office, the mention of a surgeon causes me to flashback to the memory of that first timeline.

"We'll cut it off just above the hip." The surgeon had smiled at us as though he'd delivered some good news, something other than the dismemberment he'd described. On hearing his accent, I immediately suspected that he was only visiting on a walkabout, working temporarily at this hospital just to get a quick glimpse at the beauty of Victoria before leaving, as did so many of the Australians I'd met. It wasn't until he explained further that I realized a person in his position couldn't possibly have been brought in short term.

Wyatt managed a smile. "That's no problem. I'll just get one of those artificial legs."

"You won't be able to get a prosthetic, mate" the doctor replied, his tone too casual. "You've been referred to me because I specialize in surgical oncology. You'll be getting a high leg amputation; I have to take the hip with it." He didn't so much as skip a beat before saying, "It means you'll be in a wheelchair for the rest of your life."

Wyatt's smile disappeared and the office became so silent you could hear the ticking of the big white wall clock over his head. It should've been painted black. His fingers gripped Emily's hand with a tightness that took the place of cursing, took the place of collapsing. There was only silence as Wyatt imagined the life ahead of him, his eyes looking past the doctor at the bare wall behind him.

He was holding on to what he loved, crippled not by an operation but by the thought of sentencing Emily to a life caring for an invalid… or worse yet, the thought of losing her.

I felt the emotion pouring out from everyone in that moment, thick in the cold of the room.

"Well, why don't we go ahead and check out those scans," the doctor suggested. Only later did I think it odd that he had not looked at them prior to seeing us. Looking back on it all these years later, the word "unprofessional" comes to mind.

The tumor was already six inches wide by the time of our referral to this specialist, hidden inside of Wyatt's right hip. Even the doctor's smile vanished when he began to review the images. The man from down under had made a mistake by counseling us before he had done his review.

"Maybe I should've checked these out before we met," his nervousness almost caused him to laugh. "Based on these, and the way that the tumor has infiltrated the bone structure, surgery isn't possible."

"What do you mean?" There was a tremor in Emily's voice as she spoke.

"Well," the doctor answered, not meeting our eyes, "after looking at these scans, there's nothing that can really be done here. It's even spread to his lungs." He pointed to the image. "I'd say focus on a high quality of life instead, and comfort ..."

"Comfortable?" Margaret's voice was low. "With one leg?"

"You misunderstand me," the doctor nodded to her in an attempt at courtesy, his voice light. "He'll keep both of his legs. Operating would be futile and dangerous, at this point." Then he looked directly at Wyatt. "I estimate ..." he had the decency to pause, "I estimate that you have about a year to live."

Up until this point Wyatt had remained quiet, ever since the doctor had told him that he would spend the rest of his life in a wheelchair. With this new information, he exploded. "What the hell are you talking about?" He fumbled for words. "I just turned 21!" The doctor nodded. I looked at Wyatt and noticed the streak of a tear making its way down his left cheek. Margaret had joined him, but Emily and I remained stoic.

Wyatt vented his fury upon the doctor for several moments that were frozen in time, perhaps it was seconds or possibly minutes. All the while tears streamed down his face as he came to terms with his mortality, or more correctly the announcement that his life would not be long. To his credit, the doctor just listened until Wyatt had nothing left; no fury and no more tears.

*****

We left the office without words while the world crumbled around us. Margaret shook in the passenger's seat of the car with sobs that revealed the rawness in her throat.

My muscles were so tense that my body throbbed, my own eyes hot enough to threaten my vision of the road. Wyatt was now mute as I looked at him in the rearview mirror.

Like me, Emily had remained impassive throughout the ordeal. I may have misjudged her feelings had I not overheard what I did, the conversation held faintly under the noise of Margaret battling her tears.

"Emily," Wyatt's whisper was hoarse. "I… I can't do this to you."

I kept my eyes on the road, but it was impossible not to listen.

"When we get home, you don't have to stay with me. We should split up. I don't want you to have to live this way."

Emily was silent.

"Even if I make it through this… I don't know what I'll be at the end." Wyatt's whisper was painful.

There was a long pause. When Emily finally answered, her voice was so low I could hardly hear her, "Are you crazy?" she murmured. The hum of tires on pavement was the only sound. "…I love you. We are going to get through this together."

It was a long time before Wyatt answered, and he spoke loudly enough that Margaret raised her head. "We're going to kick its ass."

Even Emily didn't realize how much her devotion would be tested. She and Wyatt had been inseparable since the day they had met four years earlier, and she loved him with an absolute dedication that he never once stopped returning, even as the pain gripped him.

All these years later I have tried to imagine what must have gone through Emily's mind when she heard that the man she loved, the man she intended to spend her life with, had been issued a death sentence.

That was the day we all began to fight back… in that old life, long *before* Stonehenge gave us a second chance.

\*\*\*\*\*

*I'm not going to let it happen again*, I think to myself, still sitting in Doctor Markham's office. The biggest difference

I notice between that old timeline and this one is that there are no tears in the room.

"It requires a surgeon," says the doc.

"What?" I ask. In this reality, the white clock is over her head, and it tells me how long my reverie lasted.

Everyone turns to look at me, and I suddenly feel like a schoolboy caught daydreaming in class.

Wyatt smiles "Dad, haven't you been listening? We've been talking about the biopsy for the last five minutes. What did you think we were talking about?"

"Sorry. I just sort of zoned out."

The doctor continues. "If it is cancer, it's stage one at most. You'll likely need radiation, chemo, and then an operation to remove it."

*Yes, an operation.* I think...*but he will not get an amputation. I'm here to make sure that never happens. Two years from now Wyatt is going to be healthy, walking around on two good legs and busy growing old with Emily,* I vow silently.

*History will not repeat itself.*

# Part Three – The First Timeline

*History will not repeat itself, I had vowed while sitting in the doctor's office.*

*You are probably wondering, "What was that history?"*

*Let me tell you what happened, what I remember, and about the journey we took...back when we first lived all of this - in the timeline that existed before Stonehenge rewound the clock.*

# Christmas Day

*\* 2013 \**

After the toll of nearly a month in the hospital, I was shocked when Wyatt and Emily still insisted on hosting Christmas dinner in their new apartment. After Wyatt's illness and Emily's dedication, none of us could bring ourselves to protest and by the time I arrived late on that holiday afternoon I had settled myself for a quiet, none-too-festive occasion.

A wreath on the door surprised me and I smiled, proud of even that effort. But when the door to the apartment opened, I found myself transfixed. Somehow, Emily had found the energy and the time to create Christmas. Fir garlands were strung across the walls, filling the room with the sweet scent of pine and culminated in a full, vibrant tree, gently glowing in its own corner. Sprigs of holly decorated the tabletops and miniature snowy villages and Santa Clauses nestled in among the usual antiques. Hanging over the chaise lounge chair Wyatt had occupied almost permanently since returning home was a bough of mistletoe.

"This is incredible," I exclaimed, and Margaret appeared in the doorway between the kitchen and living room.

"I know," she replied, and her eyes shone briefly. "Their first Christmas in their own place. Can you believe it?" I struggled to smile and couldn't find a reply.

"Come into the kitchen," she suggested. "We're just waiting on Taylor and Anthony."

When we passed through the doorway, my smile returned unbidden. The kitchen, already small, was even smaller than normal - filled with the smell of cinnamon and other mysterious spices. Peggy frowned at a saucepan on the stove and added a generous dash of a spice I didn't recognize. Wyatt's walker was backed into a corner and he sat on it laughing with a red blanket tucked over his legs as Emily approached him with a spoon.

"Just try it," she teased, and he wrenched his head away.

"I'm not having that crap," he was laughing through his protests, "anything but quinoa!" But Emily found him with the spoon and he swallowed manfully, pulling a grimace a tad too exaggerated to be real.

"Okay," he said after a moment, "what's that again?"

"Stuffing," Emily smiled. "Completely vegetarian."
Wyatt's nose wrinkled.

"Fine, I admit it, the stuff is good. But remind me why we're not just eating normal stuffing?" Before Emily could answer, he'd seen me. "Hey, Santa Pops!"

"Merry Christmas, Wyatt. Congratulations on living in the most perfectly decorated apartment on the island!"

"Isn't it incredible?" he exclaimed. "Emily and Peggy did it all while I was sleeping."

"It wasn't too hard given that he slept a good twenty hours once he was back in his own bed. He's almost back to his normal self again!" Peggy set down her saucepan and ambushed me with a hug that I awkwardly accepted.

"Pops," Wyatt said dramatically, "you are not going to believe what Emily is making me do. I thought life couldn't get worse than the food in the hospital until I came home and found my refrigerator had been pillaged!"

"You agreed to this," Emily protested, and greeted me with a smile.

"Word," Wyatt grumbled.

"We're trying a plant-centered diet. My mom read in a book that the holistic approach can really work wonders on chemo symptoms and cancer, and I figured anything to make Wyatt feel better!"

"Actually, Emily," Peggy interjected, "I read that the vegan lifestyle can stop cancer on its own without chemotherapy poisoning the body." Emily rolled her eyes.

"Well, we're giving the combination a go, so we should be unstoppable. Actually, despite what Wyatt says, the food is actually pretty good. Here, try it!" She extended the spoon to me, and, unable to think of an excuse, I took it. Wyatt laughed loudly at my expression.

"That's what I said, Pops."

Combined with the carols floating in the air and the expression on my son's face, I thought it was one of the most delicious things I'd ever tasted.

By the time we had stuffed ourselves with home-cooked, albeit vegetarian holiday foods and opened gifts, the light from the windows was deepening and the lights twinkling on the Christmas tree were becoming more pronounced with each passing minute.

# The Butchart Gardens

When Robert and Jennie Butchart came to live at Tod Inlet on Vancouver Island they named their home 'Benvenuto'— Italian for 'Welcome'.

Starting with sweet pea seeds and a rose bush, Jennie began a lifelong project to create a garden. With great vision, she transformed the barren limestone quarry (excavated to supply the cement factory nearby).

Now, 55 acres of breathtaking gardens on the 130 acre estate are visited by close to a million people each year. In 2004, during our 100th anniversary, The Butchart Gardens, still family owned, was designated a National Historic Site of Canada

– Butchart Gardens brochure

*Dec.31, 2013 *

By New Year's Eve – his and Emily's five-year anniversary - Wyatt still struggled, and depended on crutches and a walker to get around. Driving was impossible, so when he told Margaret and me that he wanted to take Emily to Butchart Gardens for their celebration we had little idea as to how it would work. Emily didn't drive, having been raised without need of a car, but Wyatt was insistent that the date had to be "special." It would be one of the last opportunities they had to spend time together before his next series of chemo would start. Doctor Markham had made it clear to us that this break between treatments was the best he would feel for quite some time.

It was ultimately Wyatt's grandmother who came up with the idea to have me act as the young couple's chauffeur, and Margaret had me take her car because it was larger than Wyatt's and, of course, the leather seats were heated. I dressed myself in a suit and tie and even a chauffeur's cap, determined to look the part. When I arrived at their apartment, I made my way around the car to be ready to open the passenger doors and was struck breathless by the bone-chilling cold. I couldn't remember a night in Victoria with this weather, but I gritted my teeth. Thankfully, Margaret had stocked the back seats with blankets, thermoses of hot chocolate, and an abundance of snacks. She'd wanted to fill it with flowers, as well, but I'd protested that if any place in the world didn't need more flowers, it was Butchart Gardens.

I was only at the door for a few seconds when they exited their own apartment. Despite his crutches, Wyatt extended his forearm to Emily and she held it lightly as they descended the stairs. She was likely supporting him as much as he was trying to be a gentleman, but they made quite the debonair couple together. With the break from treatment Wyatt had finally been able to fit into his suit again, and he was wrapped in an elegant cashmere coat that I had lent him just that morning—the coat I would have been wearing, had I not given it away. Emily was swathed in layers of scarves over a smart black dress hidden under a long beige jacket.

"Hey, Pops," Wyatt grinned when they reached the bottom of the stairs.

"Good evening, Sir, Madam." I lifted my cap. "I'll be your chauffer this evening. You'll find your seats well equipped with amenities, but please don't hesitate to ask me for anything you may need." I opened the door for them and offered my gloved hand for assistance as they lifted themselves into the car, laughing at my grave face. I was, however, determined to play my part.

"Where to, Sir?" I asked, though I knew the destination.

"It's a surprise, Jeeves." Wyatt laughed and I struggled not break my character. For the rest of the night, I was Jeeves the Chauffer.

Twenty-eight minutes into the drive, the Gardens came into view. I heard Emily gasp from the back seat and couldn't help a sigh of appreciation myself.

The entirety of the park was decked in lights visible from a mile away, every tree wrapped in bulbs and every garden path lined with lanterns. Several brilliant Christmas trees studded the park and the restaurant at the top of the hill glowed warmly. I parked the car in the handicapped space.

"This is perfect," I heard Emily whisper. It was.

"Alright, Jeeves, enjoy your evening." Wyatt assumed a posh accent and looked delighted when Emily laughed. "I'll give you a call when we're near done."

I nodded my acknowledgement and waited at the car until they had disappeared into the glow of light around the gate to the park. Wyatt was on crutches, still wearing my black cashmere overcoat topped off with a black knit hat extending over his ears. Emily had absolutely nothing to keep her head warm but the red of her hair. I returned to the driver's seat, pulled out a book and positioned my phone just next to my thigh.

It was nearly three hours before my mobile finally rang and I was startled by the sound. As they arrived back at the car I held the door open, first for Lady Emily - while Wyatt remained patiently perched on his crutches - and then for Master W himself.

"Well, Jeeves," Wyatt grinned, "I think the evening has been successful. After begging all through dinner, the lady has finally agreed to love me for another year."

"Wyatt!" Emily laughed in protest and I closed the doors, feeling thoroughly warm for the first time that evening.

"Jeeves," Wyatt called when I was in my seat, "we would like to make a brief visit to my mother's place, to wish her a Happy New Year. I assume you know the way?"

"Of course Master Wyatt."

However, when I assumed that they would be brief in their visit, I was mistaken. After assuring them it was not my place as a chauffeur to accompany them inside, I spent nearly half an hour shivering at the car door, certain that at any moment they'd be ready to go and realize I'd been waiting for them, like a true professional.

When they finally emerged and found me where they'd left me, I was a few shades bluer. However, their smiling faces brought me all the warmth I needed.

# An Invitation

*\* February 3, 2014 \**

"It's happening Dad!" The words came out of Wyatt's mouth fast and loud, as if they were shot from a cannon.

"What?" I looked over at the clock before returning to the phone call. "It's six in the morning. Are you okay? What's happening?"

Wyatt snickered. "Sorry to call you so early, but I've just been invited to play the biggest show on Earth."

I wiped the sleep from my eyes and sat up in my bed. "What show?"

"Glastonbury Festival. I've been invited to perform there."

I wasn't as excited as my son was, and with no coffee, my words came out far slower. "Glaston-what?"

Wyatt laughed. "It's like the raddest venue in electronic dance music ... a quarter of a million sweaty ass people grooving to the beats. It's in England."

That did sound pretty damn awesome, but my feet were still on Earth unlike Wyatt's. "What about your treatment? Don't you think you should focus on that?"

"I'm pretty sure I'm cured ... or at least in remission. This chemo Markham is giving me is really working. I can almost walk without crutches. Aside from yakking from the medicine she gives me, I feel great, one hundred per cent.

Plus, the tour isn't for another four months. If I feel this great now, imagine how I'll feel then. Now that I think about it, chemo will be over. I've already done four rounds. One or two more to go." He paused and I could tell he was thinking about what the Australian surgeon had told him back in September. "If surgery happens, it'll have to be after my tour."

I thought about the Aussie's words and shivered in spite of my warm bed. Then my thoughts came back to what Wyatt and I were discussing. "Tour?"

"Yes, the date at Glastonbury is part of a full tour my record label is putting together for me over in the United Kingdom. Six weeks. Dad, the DJ Lewd Behavior has arrived. My music is charting, I'm getting lots of remixing work …. Though I haven't been able to accept most of it because of the treatment. This tour will solidify my reputation as a world-class DJ. In the electronica world, being invited to Glastonbury is like being invited to the Academy Awards."

Yes, I felt old. I just did not understand electronic dance music. Regardless, I knew this was a big moment for my son. "Congratulations Wyatt… or should I say congratulations to 'Lewd Behavior'."

# Valentine's Day

*\* February 14th, 2014 \**

As fluffy white blossoms appeared on the cherry trees, and lovers exchanged cards and red boxes of chocolates, optimism sank into our bones as though seeping through with the sun as it headed toward spring. True to Dr. Markham's reassurances, chemotherapy had changed everything. Wyatt was walking again with the aid of forearm crutches, and with nearly full mobility he was able to live an almost normal life.

With a clear head and a body free of pain, Wyatt began to realize he was soon going to live the life he had only dreamed of. Not a single conversation went by that didn't mention "Glasto", or "my U.K. tour." It was an affirmation that, despite everything he was going through, he was making his mark on the world doing what he loved: music.

It was amidst this wellspring of positivity that a review of a new CT scan was scheduled. "Well, you never know, but I'd be surprised if this chemo wasn't successful," Dr. Markham had told us, revealing a rare glimmer of hope.

*****

As we assembled in her office, a week after those scans, the doctor was her usual professional self. "It's nice to see you looking so healthy, Wyatt." She nodded to Emily and me as we entered an examination room at the clinic. "I've been studying your results." I noticed the shadow on Wyatt's face when she didn't immediately reassure him. "How have you been feeling?"

"Totally awesome!" Wyatt smiled and shot her two thumbs up with his fingers still on the handgrips of the crutches as he sat down in a big leather recliner.

"I'm glad to hear it. Now, I don't want anyone to panic," Dr. Markham said slowly, "but it looks as though this treatment has not been as effective as we might have hoped. The cancer has still spread. Certainly more slowly than it may have without treatment, but nowhere near what I would have expected."

"What does this mean?" Wyatt's voice was panicked. "What will it mean for my tour?"

"Well, what it means as far as treatment goes is that I'd suggest we continue chemotherapy, but step it up a notch. We need to be as aggressive as this cancer is. I still hope to put a stop to the spread of the cancer… for as long as possible."

"The hope?" I asked, and Dr. Markham didn't meet my eyes.

"Okay," Wyatt said, "but what about my tour? How does this treatment schedule in? Can I take the time off for the trip?"

"That may be a good idea," the doctor said slowly. "I don't want you to spend your life on this chemo, especially if it's… well, if it doesn't seem likely to change the outcome."

Wyatt's face was pure relief, so focused on performing that he hardly seemed to grasp the weight of what the doctor was saying… or more correctly *wasn't* saying. Emily met my eyes from across the room and I could see the bright shine of fear.

# The Ides of March

*\* March 15th, 2014 \**

The drugs brutalized Wyatt's body, so intense that the poison the doctors called "chemo" seemed to be killing him. His mantra through it all was *"Glastonbury"*; it and the love that he shared with Emily were the only things that kept him going.

When Emily called me just past midnight, three weeks into the treatment, I immediately feared the worst. "We're at the hospital," she said breathlessly. "Wyatt collapsed in the bathroom … he must have been trying to get there to throw up, he hates asking for my help—"

Less than an hour later a nurse guided me down a hall in silence, her shoes making no noise against the linoleum and all conversation replaced by the slow, steady sounds of respirators and monitors. From each door came a slow, steady beeping, the sound of fluids dripping, and patients moaning in their sleep.

I hardly recognized Wyatt when I reached his room. His head was shrunken under a knit beanie, his eyes sunken in, mouth gaping open in an attempt for air as he slept. I had to wash my hands before I was allowed to touch him.

"Wyatt," I whispered, taking his hand. I didn't want to wake him, I told myself, but I was desperate for some kind of movement, some kind of acknowledgement.

"He's out pretty heavy." A voice came from the dark corner across the room and I inhaled sharply in surprise. Emily's ginger hair emerged from a heap of blankets on a couch, the pale features of her face becoming clear.

"Sorry, I didn't mean to startle you," she sighed groggily. "They gave him a little bit of morphine."

"Emily," I looked at her in surprise. "What are you doing here?" I shouldn't have been startled because Wyatt had never spent a night alone in the hospital because of her. Before Christmas, she had spent four straight weeks sleeping on a couch next to his hospital bed.

Her smile was weary. "Where else would I be?" She rose from the sofa wearing a green sweater and gray sweat pants.

I paused. "What exactly is going on?"

"They think he's got an infection and a blood clot." She pulled a chair to the side of the bed and rested her head on the mattress, placing both her hands on Wyatt's. "They said the tumor's gotten into the artery in his right leg. It's really swollen. So they're going to have to keep him here for a while. If the clot breaks up, it could get to his lungs." She didn't need to tell me that it could be fatal. I heard her yawn, though her face was shielded as she lay against the bed. She didn't speak again as she drifted off in that awkward position.

After I was certain that Emily was asleep, I bent over the side rail of Wyatt's bed and whispered to him "You need to fight through this. It's not your time… you have a lot left to do." I looked at Em dreaming on the couch, not much more than a girl herself, "You have a young lady who's crazy about you and so much more music to make… plus you have that tour coming up, and that gig you've been dreaming of. It's going to be so awesome!"

I paused for a moment before adding, "I'm never going to leave your side until we beat this."

# He's Back

*\* March 23rd, 2014 \**

In that first week every minute that passed was a triumph, and when I finally arrived one morning to find Wyatt conscious, I thought I would collapse.

"It's really going to add to my reputation, you now?" His voice was weak but enthused as his nurse smoothed over his forearm for an IV. "I've sort of started making a name for myself over there, my record company promoted me and got my stuff in some commercials, got me some dope remixing work, and some magazine articles. It's just such an incredible opportunity, to get paid for doing what I love! Honestly," he whispered conspiratorially to the nurse, "I'd do it for free." I was relieved to hear him chuckle, with a volume that was almost normal for him.

"Wyatt," I smiled in relief. "Nice to see you awake. How are you feeling?"

"Well," he paused. "I always feel better after I yak, so that's a plus." He laughed some more.

I shook my head at him in disbelief. "Is Emily here?"

"No, I think she went for coffee. Give her a call if you want any!"

"I'm alright." Coffee was the last thing on my mind. "But we need to talk."

\*\*\*\*\*

"You are not coming!" Wyatt was livid when I told him that I was going to the United Kingdom with him. "I'm not going on tour with my Dad." His eyes which had been bright and lively just moments before were replaced by a steely glare. He was sitting up in bed ready to jump out in protest.

"I realize that you're feeling better, but something could happen and you'll need me if it does. You'll hardly even notice me. If I have to I'll fly there by myself and just hang out in the UK, on standby."

Wyatt withstood the assault on his body without complaint. This assault on his independence, however, was a devastating blow.

"Maybe it's a good idea." Emily added, holding a steaming paper cup in her hand, and I was thankful to have an ally in the room.

But even Emily's support couldn't win Wyatt over - yet. With some hidden reserve of energy, he shouted me out of the hospital room. But I had made my vows and they'd been set in motion.

By the time they returned to their apartment a few days later, I knew from his warm demeanor that he'd resolved himself to my company, and I managed to convince him that I might even be an asset.

As bitter as he may have felt towards me initially, it wasn't a feeling he could hold onto. With his body completely exhausted, pushed to the limits of what a person could endure, his only focus was on the reward of Glastonbury.

If you can make it through this treatment, you can get to the United Kingdom.

If you can get to the UK, you can survive this cancer.

If you can survive this cancer, you can do anything.

It went unspoken, but it was Wyatt's chorus. By the time the final round of chemo was finished and the last CT scan done, cancer no longer existed as far as he was concerned.

When he called me only ten days before our flight was scheduled, I naturally assumed he'd been struck with some new concern about the details of his tour, or learned something new and incredible about one of his venues. Instead, his voice was somber.

# May

*\* May15th, 2014 \**

"Hey, Dad. I just got a call from Doctor Markham. I'd asked her not to give me information on the CT scan until I got back from the tour, but she called me about it anyways."

As I stood on a busy downtown street with the sun setting, cell phone in hand, my eyes were fixed on a Japanese cherry tree whose blossoms had withered. I did my best to breathe steadily. "Okay, so what exactly did she say?"

"There's something new growing in my lower spine." Then he laughed as if what he said was ridiculous. "She wants me to cancel my tour."

*****

Wyatt had finally been free of chemo, free to be nothing but a musician - up-and-coming, and headed to one of the most prestigious music festivals in the entire world. Now he was back to being a patient. I felt like something had died – realizing at that moment how important his dream was to all of us.

I should have known the thought, as painful as it was to me, was completely intolerable to Wyatt. That afternoon, as I stared numbly out the window of my most recent hotel room, I received another call from him.

"Pops?" His voice was shaking and my muscles instinctively tensed.

"What's going on?" I was prepared to dial 9-1-1.

"Dad," he chuckled, "my tour is on."

I stared at the phone briefly, disoriented. "How is that possible? Wyatt, you know we all want this for you, but you need treatment."

"Yeah, yeah, I know." He laughed, because this was Wyatt and life was good. "I've been on the phone with Dr. Markham. She's been talking to some of her peeps - I mean people- at the center … I can get aggressive radiation. So, like, the full dosage, but in a shorter amount of time. If I get that treatment ASAP, I can go. We can still go!" There was a pause as he waited for my reply, but I was too stunned. "Max radiation up until I leave, right to that tumor in my spine."

"You're going to have intense radiation on your spine just before you board a ten-hour flight? That sounds crazy."

"I'll feel like crap for the first few days, but then I'll feel fine. Besides, if I could get through that last chemo I can get through anything."

I looked out my window again, the lights of the city coming in and out of focus amidst the rain. "When will you start?"

"Tomorrow."

# A Party with a Special Guest

*\* May26th, 2014 \**

A banner announced the purpose of the family gathering at Margaret's house. At this time tomorrow Wyatt, Emily and I would be on a flight to London, and this was our "Going Away" party.

Margaret had prepared a feast for the occasion. For Wyatt, Taylor, Anthony and I there was peppercorn beef tenderloin, and for Emily a juicy salmon steak.

However, it turned out that we were not the stars of this evening - for it was on this night that we opened the time capsule we had made as a family over a dozen years ago.

\*\*\*\*\*

A thousand years from now future generations will remember the paranoia surrounding the change of the millennium to the year 2000. They will snicker as they remember us for our belief that disaster would befall us because of the two-digit year programmed into our computers. One myth was that upon the change from 1999 to 2000, airplanes would fall from the sky. Another was that power grids would fail and we would return to the dark ages. Would our computers even work anymore? Would the internet, which was still in its infancy, survive? The shocking reality was that *nothing happened* on the advent of the new millennium. It was against this background that our family had created a time capsule on December 31, 1999.

We were living in the deep south at the time, in a place where (as the residents describe it) Louisiana meets Arkansas and Mississippi. The experiences of crawfish, alligators, and bayous were foreign and exciting to my family. My job at a local telephone company had brought us down from Canada.

The time capsule was a shiny red cylinder that was a yard long and a foot wide. Everyone in our family contributed objects to it. As the years went by, we could only faintly remember what was in it. It was supposed to stay sealed until New Year's Eve of 2019, but due to Wyatt's condition, we decided to open it as part of these going-away festivities.

*****

After we cleared the dishes, Margaret emerged from her storage room with a long red object. Wyatt, back scorched by radiation and bald head, smiled as he recognized what she was carrying and announced it. "Fifteen years later, the family is un-wrapping their time capsule" Then he reminisced "… things were very different back when I was a kid."

Margaret removed the cover and the first thing she found inside was Pikachu's smiling face.

# Pokémon and Ancient Gum

*\* May 26th, 2014 \**

The happy face of bright yellow Pikachu peered at us from the cover of an old Pokémon Guide.

"Are you for real?" Wyatt said. Then he turned to Emily who was silently observing, "This is like my seventh birthday party all over again, babe." She smiled back at him – happy to see him happy.

Then Margaret pulled out a Pokémon trading card. "It's Beedrill", I commented. The species was a bee with a yellow and black striped tail that resembled a drill. The information printed on it gave its length as 3'3" and a weight of 65 pounds. "Not the type of bee you want to be stung by." I said by way of understatement. We all laughed, remembering the craze that overtook the kids back then.

As I handed the card to Wyatt, we fumbled the exchange. The radiation had weakened him so much that he couldn't get out of his chair to retrieve it, so I did it for him. "I'm going to start rebuilding my collection," he said.

From the tube I pulled out another Pokémon card.

"Oh, a good one", Wyatt said, "Vaporeon". Its picture looked like a cross between a baby blue seal, a fish, and a dragonfly. Around its neck was an Elizabethan collar, just like the one Shakespeare wore. "Did we put any full packs of hockey cards in?" Wyatt used to collect those too. "Shoddy the gum if it's still there."

I was sure that no one was going to argue with him over an old stick of gum

"There's some weird stuff in there," Taylor observed as I extracted an old cassette tape.

The next item was a small child's handprint "We have to figure out whose this is? Put your hand here," I said to Wyatt, and he played along with the gag by putting his huge hand against it. Then I brought it over to Anthony and said in a musical voice "its Anthony's ..." Acting like it fit, but it was miniature compared to his of course. Finally, I brought it over to Taylor and she gingerly placed her hand over it "Its Taylor's." She had the smallest hand, though it still didn't nearly match that of the little girl who made it. "It's pink. It must be yours." Without saying anything, Taylor took possession of it. Case closed.

As I continued to pull the contents out, I extracted an unopened pack of O-Pee-Chee hockey trading cards, 1991-92 season. This was what Wyatt was looking for, so I handed it to him.

"I'm opening it." As he began to unwrap it I didn't wait to see if he would actually eat the two-decade-old gum.

"This may be the coolest thing," I said dramatically as I waved an unspectacular looking piece of paper in the air. The fireplace in the corner crackled as the room hushed. "Predictions made by each and every one of us made back in 1999." I paused for dramatic effect, "Anthony's prediction:" I announced with a flourish. He was busy on his smart phone and struggled to get back into the scene.

Before I could state the prediction Wyatt announced, "I ate the gum."

This stunned the group into silence as everyone considered the grossness of chewing on two-decade-old gum. Then Taylor broke the silence and pointed to him in glee "ha, ha, ha!"

"No, no, no. I ate the gum in 1999." The room exploded with laughter as we all realized Wyatt was going to be okay. "What a rip off," he added. It took a minute for the chuckling to subside.

"Would you have eaten it?" His little sister asked through her laughter.

"I wanted to" Wyatt answered sincerely.

After the room quieted, I stood up in the middle and said "The next prediction, from Anthony." Reading from the old paper, "Little aliens called 'Bing Bongs' will have tried to take over the Earth, and we bing-bonged them back to where they belong." His mother clapped her hands together in delight.

"He's right," Wyatt chuckled. "It happened!" Then with a wide grin, he turned to Anthony, "Did you turn into a Bing Bong?"

Anthony of course denied it, but a suspicious gaze overtook Wyatt's face as he studied him.

While I rummaged through the time capsule Wyatt scanned the room from left to right and said, "I'm so lucky" as he took a sip from a can of ginger ale… the drink that helped ward off the nausea that had plagued him during the mega-radiation sessions of the past week.

Next, I pulled out a video game.

"Nice," Wyatt said as I handed it to him. "For N64 dude! Oh, ho, ho, ho, ho." he sounded a bit like Santa Claus. "Whoa. That's old school," he said referring to the old gaming console.

Then I pulled out some family photos - Halloween in Louisiana with Wyatt dressed as Robin Hood and Taylor dressed as a medieval princess. The costumes were hand sewn by their mother. Another was of Anthony as a child holding infant Wyatt who was stylishly dressed in a tuxedo like baby outfit. Anthony's smile was brilliant, while Wyatt looked uncomfortable. Margaret passed the picture onto Wyatt who giggled at how cute the two were in the picture.

A procession of trinkets, memorabilia, artifacts and goofball toys followed until Wyatt picked up the empty time capsule and peered into it, "All done." He then suggested we make a new one. "I'm going to put stuff in that I'm going to miss, that I'm going to want in 15 minutes." Then he said in a future he-man voice, "Yessss!" and pounded his fist on his knee, "That's where I put it!" We all laughed at the image, but the idea did not take hold.

It was getting late by this time. "I propose a toast," I said holding my wine glass in the air. Everyone did likewise with whatever drink they had. "To Wyatt and Emily and to Lewd Behavior's first international tour."

Glasses, bottles, and cans tapped in agreement.

A long journey lay ahead of us.

# Shindig Weekender

Shindig Weekender Festival is a glorious mash up of a gig, a house party, a circus show, comedy night, a wellbeing retreat and a kid's party. No main stages, just a beautiful arrangement of stretch marquees, so you can be in amongst it, or sitting on the grass supping something cold. And your kids can be learning to DJ – scratching, mixing, breakdancing and spraying paint, Each area has been carefully curated to pique its audience's interest and make it impossible to move on."

- Shindig Weekender official web page

*\* June 1, 2014 \* a farmer's field near Bath, England*

The ground was soggy and the air felt wet. The grass was the kind of green that only comes with buckets of rainfall for umpteen nights. I could hear music all around me and the din of a large crowd of people as I approached the massive circus tent set up in the middle of a forest just south of the old Roman town of Bath, located between the metropolis' of London and Bristol.

On our journey to get to this music festival, the manmade formation of rocks known as Stonehenge suddenly thrust upward from the plain as we traversed a hill.

"Man…I want to see that." Wyatt had muttered from his seat one row in front of me on the record company's tour bus.

We were at the Shindig Weekender, the first venue of the tour, and it was finally Wyatt's time – he would perform after one of the world's most famous DJ's, a man in his early thirties known as Jean-Paul. It made Wyatt nervous for about two seconds. He was already on stage and more than ready. As I entered the tent, I noticed a sign over the door proclaiming that this place was "Beyond the Stars" in large space age fonts.

Wyatt had walked through the mud with the aid of crutches, his back still stinging from the radiation treatment that seemed like a million years ago, but had only ended a week earlier. Being here was almost surreal. The ten-hour flight to London was thankfully without incident.

Inside the tent, bright lights of every color flashed from all sides and even from above. I thought I would feel out of place here, but there were people of all ages, races, and occupations. Hundreds, or maybe even thousands of people, it was hard to tell. All I could see was a sea of bodies ahead of me. Some of the people had painted their faces, while others wore costumes. One lady's entire body was painted gold. The weather was cool, so many wore jackets just like me. I squeezed through the crowd to get towards the stage where Wyatt had set up his gear.

"Our next act is coming in from across the pond," the British MC's voice boomed out over the pit, "bringing us some prime remixes to close out the Shindig. Give it up for Lewd Behavior!"

The bass came in, heavy and seductive. The drums picked up the beat, synthesizers started to squelch, and overdubbed voices that I know to be friends of Wyatt rapped about "Lewd Behavior" in their melodic Jamaican accents. I saw the sweat beading on Wyatt's brow as he cranked up the tempo. I felt movement in the air, and the crowd began to feel it too. He threw one glance off to the side of the stage, for Emily, and I could see it in his face: the thrill, the awe, the adrenaline rush.

The roar of the crowd swelled as Wyatt's music began to hum around the edges of the pit and increase in volume. I felt my chest swell as I saw, for a brief moment, Wyatt, as I had known him before the illness, transformed and transforming others with the thrill of his music. With headphones on a cranium of peach fuzz, as his arms and body swayed, he adjusted and mixed music until it became a wave that could not be resisted – that's when the place erupted into dance.

However, it was not the type of dancing I knew from my younger days - most of them were *shuffling*. I don't know how it got that name, because I didn't see a shuffle in any of the moves. I admired the dancing though. I also saw few people kicking it up *gangnam style,* a dance that resembles a person riding on a horse.

"Between 100 and 174 beats per minute." Wyatt had once told me of the music's tempo.

Within the space of a one-hour show, the suffering and pain that Wyatt had experienced during the previous six months evaporated.

The next evening, as a cricket game played out on an old television mounted on the wall of a pub in downtown Bristol, Wyatt raised his beer stein in the air and said,

"A toast to a crazy sold-out show, to a hell of an introduction to the UK, and to learning experiences in the mud, to a little extra bedding and to sleeping like babies," he paused for breath, "to a few hundred sweaty-ass people feeling the flow of the funk on the dance floor. Last, but not least, to being officially on tour. Bottoms up!"

Emily, five new friends they had made, and myself raised our glasses to his, just as we had after opening the time capsule a week earlier.

# After the Shindig

*\* June 3, 2014 \* Bristol, England*

As soon as Emily walked Wyatt into the breakfast hall of our hotel, the Tuesday after Shindig Weekender, I knew the day was off. Wyatt had deep purple shadows under his eyes and he was leaning heavily against Emily's shoulder. He looked out of place next to Emily, her red hair in a neat braid that rested on the floral scarf she'd put over a smart navy dress.

"Bad night?" I asked, trying to keep my tone light as I shifted my newspaper off the table and pulled out Wyatt's chair.

"You could call it that." Wyatt's voice was faint, but I could see he had no intention of complaining.

"I'll go get us some food," Emily said firmly, and although I wasn't feeling particularly hungry after my morning coffee, I followed and picked up one of the heated plates myself.

"Was he throwing up?" I asked with a low voice.

"No." She didn't look at me as she managed to reach for the toaster while balancing two plates. "He was tossing and turning all night." She stopped suddenly, turned to look at me, not caring whether Wyatt knew we were talking about him or not.

"There's something wrong with his back." She watched my face, waiting for a response.

"Well, he's had that radiation, no wonder he can't get comfortable…" I trailed off. "He also danced like a crazy man during his show, that didn't help."

"No," she shook her head. "Something different. He was sleeping fine. Starting to, anyways. This is something else…" It was her turn to trail off and I did my best to be comforting.

"The doctor warned that the dosage of radiation could take a while to wear off, Emily. It's just a shame Wyatt hasn't been an exception. I assume we won't be heading to the Bristol Zoo today?"

She shook her head and turned back to the plates. The two meals were starkly different. On what I presumed to be her plate, a piece of toast sat next to an apple and a single-serving package of peanut butter. On the other, another piece of toast topped with a small scoop of eggs and a single piece of bacon sat next to a relative mountain of green melon. She saw me staring.

"He can hardly eat and I'm doing whatever I can to get protein into him. He says honeydew is the only thing he's really been able to taste in a while. A side effect or something."

I followed her back to the table, forgetting my empty plate on the buffet. Wyatt ate the melon. The toast and the bacon went untouched.

# Journey to Glastonbury

Emily and Wyatt spent the day alone in their room. The few times I tried to check on them after breakfast I found the lights out, Wyatt in a fitful sleep, and Emily curled into a chair reading by the faint light coming in through the window. In whispered insistence she told me to go and see the city, find out what attractions there might be that required less walking than the zoo. She assumed we wouldn't make it there.

I spent the day alone wandering Bristol, telling myself I could scout out pubs and museums for when Wyatt was recovered. But even when I looked up from the cobblestones, my mind stayed blank, places and names slipping from me like water off a leaf. Everything was blank.

If he wasn't feeling better tomorrow, I was going to take him to the hospital.

# In the Garden of Eden

Eden Festival is a truly energetic, vibrant & independent boutique festival showcasing fresh music & electrifying performances. Set in the stunning Raehills Meadows [of Scotland] & hosting a kids arena, circus tent, drive in cinema, comedy, cabaret & workshops, as well as a feast of performers, artworks, games & much, much more...

- Official Eden Festival web page

*\* June 7, 2014 \* Moffat, Scotland*

When Wyatt returned from the breakfast buffet with haggis, Scotland's famous (infamous) dish, I said nothing as he devoured it.

"This is really good," he remarked. I was delighted to see him so hungry after he could hardly eat just a few days earlier.

I looked at Emily who was trying to stifle laughter. She looked at me and broke down.

"What's so funny?" Wyatt asked looking up at her from his steaming plate of onion, oatmeal, spices and parts of a sheep - the heart, liver, and lungs encased in the sheep's stomach.

"Nothing," Emily quickly went back to eating an assortment of fruit laid out on her own plate.

Wyatt looked at me and I smiled back. "What's going on?" he chuckled.

"It's just nice to see that you've got your appetite back."

"This is damn savory." He returned to his feast, imbibing huge forkfuls of it, while Emily and I continued to exchange humor filled glances at each other.

"This town is so beautiful," Emily said as she peeled back a banana. "This is the just about the prettiest place I've ever seen. Wyatt and I are going to explore some of the shops before we go to the festival."

The prior night we had been welcomed to the Scottish town of Moffat by the ringing of church bells on the hour, and we spent the night in this stately 18$^{th}$ Century stone mansion designed by John Adams, one of Scotland's most famous architects. The town itself got its name from the Moffats, a powerful clan that rode into battle with William Wallace, better known as Braveheart.

As breakfast at the inn continued, I decided it was time to tell Wyatt what haggis was. "Wyatt, do you know what you're eating?"

He politely finished chewing before he answered "Haggis. I know what it is by the way, so you two can just cut out the snickering. It's really delicious, you ought to try it."

*****

# Journey to Glastonbury

"What can you tell us about the Eden Festival, Alphonse?" Wyatt asked as we waited for the other performers to join us on the Skid Row Records Tour Bus.

His afro rippled as he twisted to face us. "Let's see, then. We get about five thousand in the crowds, so nothing massive like Glastonbury will be, but the energy is great. Great to perform, great to be a part of, all in this lovely meadow about ten miles from here. Should be a grand time." A short while later we were on the road.

It never seemed to dry out in this part of the world. Although it was daytime, the sky seemed unnaturally dark, the clouds effectively blocking out our sense of time. We were hushed, solemn, although heading towards the faint beating pulse of music. There was a stark difference between the cozy charm of the town and the fierce whispers of wind in the grass that spread out from us in every direction.

"When we checked the place out yesterday they still hadn't even finished the stage," Wyatt muttered nervously. "It's gonna be an interesting time."

When we came over the crest of the hill looking down into the bowl of the festival, it felt for a moment as if the sun had burst out. The music spiked in volume, echoing off the sides of the grassy hills, the stage tall and black in front of a massive dance floor checkered with lights in every color. We watched, speechless, as flames shot up from cannons behind the performer on stage. Even in the emptiness of the sound checks, the energy began to rise. Wyatt's face was flushed with excitement when I turned to look at him.

"Oh, yes. This is what I'm talking about."

# The Tourists

*\* June 11, 2014 \* Bristol, England*

*9:07 am*

As the days until Glastonbury became shorter, Wyatt's excitement grew, and with it our spirits. Each day he informed us of the number of sleeps until the big show. The energy in his voice belied the exhaustion of his body. Rather than press for a lot of sightseeing, he'd agreed to schedule just a few excursions. Emily and I had shared our relief at his concession, until he explained exactly where he wanted to go.

Stonehenge was an hour and a half drive, far enough to force an all-day trip but too close for a hotel. None of us had ever been there before, so we knew nothing of the terrain or accessibility for a guy on crutches, but Wyatt was insistent.

"I can't say I came to the U.K. and never saw Stonehenge. Then people will know all I did was party and perform. What're your excuses?" he demanded of Emily and me.

"We have no car," I began.

"It's kind of in the middle of nowhere," Emily added.

Wyatt held up a forceful hand. "C'mon guys, life is short. We've got to at least see it. I only have two shows in the next week and a half; that gives me plenty of recovery time if it ends up being a difficult trek."

Emily shot me the reluctant glance that Wyatt had come to recognize as surrender, and gave a whoop of excitement.

"Okay, great, because I've already bought our tickets! Pops, can you sort out a rental car?" my son urged me.

"What?" I had heard him, but fear had gripped me.

I could not hear Wyatt as he rambled on about how we "need to grab life", and "seize the day", or something cliché like that. While he attempted to persuade me to rent a car, I imagined what it would to be like – driving on the wrong side of the road, from the wrong side of the vehicle… narrow roads and strange rules. Then my optimistic stupid side showed up. "How hard can it be?"

"That's the attitude – positivity," Wyatt said under his all too familiar chuckle.

He walked out of the room on his crutches, leaving my head almost spinning, and a smile on Emily's face.

"There he is," she said softly, and followed him out of the dining hall.

# A Roller Coaster

*\* June 11, 2014 \* Driving erratically in the South of England*

*11:11 am*

The rental car's alarms went off every half minute or so, and between them was the repeated thud of the passenger side tires as I careened off the curb. It took me awhile to figure out what the alarms were about.

I was too close to an automobile on the right: Beeeeeeeep! Now too close to some object on the left. Beeeeeeeep! I approached the car in front of me too fast. Beeeeeeeep! Thud! The curb *again*.

I made a left turn (these were the easy ones), and found myself half on the sidewalk. A small lady who wore a mauve headscarf scrambled for cover as she dragged her manicured poodle with her. The car's GPS demanded a right turn, but amidst heavy traffic I panicked. The other cars were all approaching in the wrong lanes. I turned left instead, this time on the road instead of the sidewalk. On this day there would be no right turns unless traffic was absent.

"Are you on crack or what?" Wyatt chided.

I said tersely "I didn't think driving on the other side of the road would be so difficult!" Driving from what we consider the passenger's seat challenged my perspective. It was the reason I kept hitting the left curb.

As we continued, the two-way traffic boiled down into one lane as we entered a village filled with age-old buildings. It was noon, having already taken us two hours to get to this point only thirty miles away from Bristol. The alarms and the sound of tires careening off the curb hadn't abated as I watched the traffic in front of me wait for the road to clear so that they could take a turn to negotiate the shared lane. After four cars went ahead of me, it was my turn. That's when it happened.

The metallic screeching sound told me that I had not made it clear of a parked car on the left.

"Geez! You just hit that dude's car," Wyatt announced looking back over his left shoulder.

As I pulled over to the side, the driver that was behind us stopped abreast of me while his female companion rolled down her window. I rolled mine down too, though I really did not want to talk to her.

"Are you alright?" she said with a posh London accent.

I thought of my erratic driving, "I haven't been drinking," I said, in defense of the swerves I imagined she had seen. "I'm just not used to driving in the UK."

She nodded dismissively. I could almost hear her thinking, *stupid yank*.

I got out and examined my left front fender - scraped. I looked at the other car and saw the same thing on the driver's side. All of the seats inside it were empty. "Perhaps the owner is in the house?" I yelled in the direction of Wyatt and Em as I looked at the two-story Georgian manor.

A large dog came running at me as I approached the front door. Luckily, it was a golden retriever, a breed that demands love from everyone. Unbeknownst to me one of these affectionate beasts was in our future. As I rang the doorbell he licked my right hand, but no one answered.

"What are you going to do?" Emily asked when I returned.

I jotted my name and email, along with an apology, on a piece of paper and walked back to the scene of my crime. I looked down at the empty spot on the road. The victim and their car were gone - *reverse* hit and run.

I walked back to where Wyatt and Emily waited patiently. In unison they looked up at me.

"I don't want to drive anymore," I said.

# Our First Time at Stonehenge

*\* June 11, 2014 \* Amesbury, United Kingdom*

*1:24pm*

It took my companions about twenty minutes to convince me to keep driving. I had no choice, we were in the middle of some random town, and neither Emily nor Wyatt could drive. However, as soon as we saw the sandstone pillars in the distance, fascination replaced my anxiety. I cruised to a stop in the parking lot of Stonehenge.

We caught a tour at its beginning and Wyatt insisted we listen through the whole thing. Emily was interested, Wyatt so amazed that he forgot that he was on crutches, and I was content to watch them. As we walked around the circle of stones, they loomed over our heads into the sky. The guide told us that the only time of the year that people could get within the circle of stones was on the summer solstice. This was the moment that I had resolved to come back someday in the future. Little did I know that it would not happen for almost ten years, nor did I have any idea what the consequences would be.

We spent hours looking at all the different parts of the marvel, picnicking on Emily's packed lunch, before even entering the museum. Inside, the artifacts displayed in glass cases quickly absorbed Wyatt.

However, none of us kept track of the time inside the hushed halls, and when the museum announced it would close for the evening in a matter of minutes, we realized we had far overstayed our plans. Driving back now, in the dark, myself and the kids exhausted, was impossible. Paying for a bed and breakfast on the other hand was a far more appealing solution that would allow us to experience the quaintness of the nearby town of Amesbury the next day before driving back to Bristol.

# A Rodent

*\* June 18, 2014 \* Bristol Zoo*

The giant rat came out from behind a bush. He was at least hundred pounds, maybe even a lot more.

"Do you see that?" I said to Wyatt and Emily. "That's a capybara. The biggest rodent in the world. Close relative of gophers, mice, and rats." I had once had a nightmare about one of these critters gnawing off my legs. Up to until this point, I had only seen them in pictures; this guy – at the Bristol Zoo – was the first I had ever seen in real life. "It's from South America, I think."

"Looks more like a humungous Guinea Pig," observed Emily. "I wonder if they can be kept as pets. What do you think Wyatt, one of those in our living room?"

We had almost missed out on the wonders of this place, but I was thankful that we had made it here. So far, we had seen Meerkats, gorillas, and Wyatt's favorite – the sea turtles.

"Let's do it," answered Wyatt, "I could get him a little saddle too, and ride him to my gigs."

We lingered for a few minutes watching the rodent eat hay - do they even eat human legs? I wondered. Probably. At that moment, I thought of what had happened to Wyatt earlier that day and shivered in spite of the warm weather. I was almost surprised this morning when I looked out the window of our hotel to find that sun had replaced the rain of the past few weeks.

I unfolded a map of the zoo. Emily was looking over my shoulder. "Let's go see the butterfly gardens," she urged. We moved toward the glass building further down the path as I folded up the map, but I had to come to a sudden and complete stop to avoid tripping over the mother duck and her ducklings that had chosen that moment to cross the path just inches in front of my feet.

As I waited for them, I thought about how we almost never made it here.

*****

Earlier that day:

"Okay, zoo take two," Wyatt smiled as we stood on the grand front stoop of the hotel, looking down at the street from the top of a broad marble staircase. Up to this point, Wyatt had been slowly improving, his mobility increasing, albeit still on crutches. Our silent hope was almost tangible.

"Are you sure you're up for it, babe?" Emily placed a cautionary hand on his arm, likely the only person in any country who could have asked the question without upsetting him.

"Yeah," his voice still slightly irritated. "My legs just feel a little... weak, I don't know. But that's why we need to go to the zoo, right? I need to keep walking." He planted a kiss on her temple and carefully took the first step, his good foot before the other. Emily's face was still puckered with worry.

I was surprised that he was having any difficulty since he had once again been a bouncing DJ during his last performance. "Maybe we'll just do a half day," I reassured her. "We're not in any rush, we can stop for meals and coffee whenever he needs a rest."

"I guess you're right," she chewed her bottom lip, still watching Wyatt, "I just have this weird feeling about it."

Left crutch, left foot…and step with his other one. Wyatt attempted to lift his right foot and teetered for a moment. Then his left foot, the good one, collapsed under him and he tumbled down the remaining stairs.

"Oh, my god." Emily's voice came out fast and she vanished before I had even enough time to process what had happened. Wyatt lay in a heap of limbs and crutches at the bottom of the stairs, as a crowd quickly surrounded him and offered help.

"I'm okay, I'm okay," he insisted by the time I reached him. A broad-shouldered man had carefully pulled him to his feet as another woman offered him water. "Thank you, man, I'm okay." But his smile was wan and his tight grip on Emily's arm didn't escape my notice.

He did his best to walk on his crutches towards the bus stop across the street, but he struggled mightily.

# The Dancing Janners

*\* June 21, 2014 \* Plymouth, England*

I could overhear Wyatt talking to his mother on the phone.

"The drive down to Plymouth was stunning, so full of beauty! Scenic farmlands, plus we were once again with the raddest people, and it just worked out to be such a killer party." He was telling her about the next to last show of the tour, in the far south of England. "After performing at festivals with thousands of people, this was a much-welcomed return to the clubs. I played at a tiny little bar, but so awesome and we straight blew the spot up! It was amazing that I could go to a little town like that and feel so welcomed, and they were all so into it! The energy was unbelievably huge. That says something for the Janners!"

Margaret did not know what a Janner was, and neither did I until we went to Plymouth.

Wyatt answered her. "Yeah. That's what people from Plymouth call themselves. Strange nick name, eh?"

Margaret asked a question that led Wyatt to answer, "Well, the hotel room they booked us in was really "ghetto", so I upgraded us to a better one. It only cost ninety quid more though".

I still had not caught on to pounds, pence, and sterling, let alone a quid, so you could not fault Margaret for not understanding him. Wyatt clarified. "Oh. Sorry. It's like

124

pounds. I'm picking up some slang I think, just because everyone says it."

"Did you pick up a lot of quid from your performance?" I interrupted his phone call wearing a sly smirk.

"I did alright," he answered, sensing a trap.

"Good. You're buying at the pub," I kidded.

Wyatt shook his head and returned to his phone call. "Did you see the pictures I posted on the web? My hair is growing back, and I even have eyebrows again!" He chuckled and I could hear my ex laughing on the other end.

"Yeah, Mom, no injuries," Wyatt said, responding to a question about the fall he had taken a few days earlier. I had noticed that his performance at Plymouth was a little more subdued. He did try to dance as he normally does, but he could not. He propped himself up on one of the pillows on the bed. "Okay, maybe a couple bruises. But nothing broken, nothing bloodied. I'm just going to have to take it easy. It sucks, but it'll be fine. Just another side effect of the radiation, I guess. I've been doing great, otherwise."

The conversation ended with Wyatt saying to his mother, "I'm so stoked. I'll be on stage at Glastonbury in a week. Can you believe it?"

*****

I hadn't noticed two things: first, that chemo had robbed Wyatt of his eyebrows, and second that they were back. After he hung up the phone, I said, "Wyatt, let me see these bushy brows you've been bragging about." The alliteration made us both smile.

He turned to me, "Sure."

The growth above his eyes was scant, but I congratulated him on their return anyway. The hair on the top of his head was also growing, though it was still bristle short.

"I have expressions again," said Wyatt.

"I didn't realize they were gone. Okay, let me see."

Emily, who had been manicuring her nails, put the file down to watch.

"Get ready." Wyatt took a deep breath for composure and held a hotel napkin in front of his face. "Surprise!"

The napkin dropped and revealed the ridiculous arrangement of his face, intact eyebrows raised over saucer wide eyes and his mouth hanging completely open. Emily and I began to laugh.

The napkin went back up and dropped a second later. "Sad!" This time his eyebrows slanted dramatically down, his mouth drooping in despair.

He followed this with happy and angry, and it was like watching a great pantomime artist who knew how to keep his audience in stitches.

"Confused!" This final display was perhaps the funniest. Eyebrows furrowed, his head twisted side to side, lips pursed and jaw jutting forward.

The poor guy. He looked completely lost, but you can't help a confused soul when you're busy cracking up.

# A Helping Hand

*June 22, 2014 * Bristol, England*

With a tense voice, Emily had called me on the hotel phone asking me to come over as soon as possible. Their room was dim as I entered, with the drapes keeping the morning sun at bay. The only light came from the bathroom. In the darkness I noticed that Wyatt was still lying in bed, his upper body propped up by two pillows. I could see a reflection off his liquid eyes.

"What's going on?" I asked.

"Can you give me a hand, Daddio?" Wyatt replied, struggling to be positive.

"Sure." I walked over, extended my arm and offered him my hand.

"I need more help than that," he said.

I looked over at Emily who stood at the foot of his bed. "What do you need us to do, Wyatt?" she asked in a firm but calm voice.

I looked over at him for direction. "I need both of you to help me out," he answered.

I went to Wyatt's left side, the one closest to the edge of the bed. I squatted down to get an arm under his shoulder. Emily, such a tiny person, prepared to help as best she could. "Okay, slip your left leg down and I'll pull you up,"

I said, preparing to yank him out, but not really sure how this was going to work.

His words echoed around the room, bouncing off the walls, and inside my head. "I can't move my legs at all."

# The Show Must Go On

*June 23, 2014 * Bristol, England*

"I'm calling the cancer center back home," Emily announced, appearing at my door alone. "Wyatt still can't walk, or even stand. It's been almost 24 hours, and no improvement."

I stood at my desk, frowning slightly. "You know he doesn't want to be thinking about it…" I trailed off, my defenses weak. I'd been desperate to make the call myself.

"Yeah, so I won't tell him about it. Can I use your room to call?" Her jaw was set, hand already wrapped around the phone. I nodded and asked that she put it on the speaker so that I could listen.

"Can you describe the symptoms?" The doctor-on-duty asked brusquely, from several time zones and thousands of miles away. I could hear him tapping on a computer.

"There's no pain or anything, he just can't walk. Wyatt can still feel them, a little, and he can move his toes on his left leg." That last part gave us hope that the condition was temporary.

The doctor's response was terse. "He has to come home." Without reply, Emily disconnected the line. Had any other shows remained beside Glasto, maybe Wyatt would have canceled and returned home early, but the biggest show of his life loomed like Eve's apple, so close he could almost touch it.

"Well, that was helpful," she shook her head as if what the man had said was ridiculous, but her face was pale. "No chance of that. Wyatt says he *will* perform, with or without two good legs." She left the room without another word, leaving both of us to our private fears. His gig at Glastonbury Festival was four days away and we had a lot to do.

While Wyatt sat with headphones preparing the best DJ set of his young life, Emily and I watched YouTube videos demonstrating how to help a person who can't walk.

By the next day, we had rented a wheel chair. As the big day approached, it became clear that this was Wyatt's only hope.

# Avalon

Here in Somerset we keep a few surprises up our sleeve!

You'd never expect that our peaceful pastures would give rise to the world's biggest and best known long-running pop festival. But you'll find the Glastonbury Festival – Glasto to friends – springing up each June at Worthy Farm... A list of all the acts and performers who have entertained packed crowds at the five-day Glastonbury Festival reads like a roll call of modern music. Every year anything up to 200,000 people turn up to see them, creating a substantial tented city at Pilton for one week a year. Every kind of alternative lifestyle is also represented - It's a wonderful scene! The only problem is that tickets sell out in minutes, and I'm afraid we can't arrange them for you but it's quite a spectacle just being around the area.

- The official tourism website for Somerset

*June 27, 2014 * Pilton, Somerset, England*

There are *no* swimming pools at the Glastonbury Festival of Contemporary Performing Arts.

There are *no* rivers, lakes or streams either.

But … there *is* a lifeguard.

"Swim people!" he urged from high atop a tower in an area of the festival grounds known as the Fields of Avalon.

Wyatt, sitting in his wheelchair looked up at him, then left and right, and twisted to look behind him. He looked at Emily and said, "What the hell?" She shrugged her shoulders.

I had pushed Wyatt through the front gate twenty minutes earlier on our way to his gig at Glasto's Totem Gardens. He wore his baseball cap backwards at a bit of an angle, and he now sported a slight beard. To keep warm he wore long pants and a navy blue hoody emblazoned with Skid Row Records. Likewise, Emily and I were dressed for cold weather and we all wore rubber boots now, having become veterans of the UK outdoor festival experience these past six weeks.

The man atop the lifeguard stand had a different opinion of the weather. He was sheltered from the non-existent sun by a large rainbow striped parasol. His shirt was a splash of bright flowery yellow and his shorts were florescent sky blue. His eyes hid behind sunglasses, though we thought the day was dark and gloomy. His voice, amplified by a blow horn, urged us once more, "Swim people. If you're not swimming, you're drowning."

All around us, colorful flags fluttered in the wind. A hundred yards behind us, we had passed a circus tent with aerial performers flying high above the spectators.

# Journey to Glastonbury

The pool guy bellowed again, "No pushing, no shoving, and especially...." He paused and then glared directly at us with accusation etched on his face ... "NO TOUCHING!"

"Okay ...." Emily said, shaking her head. "Shall we keep moving?"

Wyatt had only been in a wheelchair for a few days, so he wasn't used to propelling it. I pushed him, thankful that the ground was dry and hoping that it would remain so despite the puffy black clouds that had assembled above us.

As we continued our journey, I could hear a crooner belt out a Sinatra song while bubbles floated through the air and across our path. A cage on wheels drove by us filled with clowns. Further down from us was the Pyramid Stage, with a hundred thousand people bunched together like sardines in a can, listening to a Mexican flamenco-rumba band. Though there aren't any places to swim at Glasto, there is a free university, a juggling school, and a drive-in theater where all of the cars are sculpted works of art.

Many of the young people I observed sported costumes, painted faces, or exotic hairstyles in a myriad of colors. However, Glasto tickets had been distributed by lottery, so there were also "normal looking" older people and parents pulling their children in wagons. On the fringes of the one square mile festival grounds were people of modest means who would spend tonight in a tent, while the wealthy flew in by helicopter and stayed in one of the luxury trailer parks just outside the main gates. Some, like us, commuted from nearby cities and towns.

As we arrived at Totem Gardens, six-foot high Easter Island heads welcomed us with their huge stone jaws jutting forward, some leaning toward us, others tilted back. Emily touched one to see if it was real. Towering wooden totem poles that looked as authentic as the ones back home surrounded a temple dedicated to electronica music. Rhythm filled the air - along with the smell of cow pies and straw that served as a reminder that this place is a working dairy farm when it is not a festival. Later today, Wyatt, aka Lewd Behavior, would perform in this temple. Tomorrow night he would play an even bigger venue – Glastonbury's Hell Stage.

Wyatt's smile was broad as he interacted with the production crew. He talked faster than normal as they discussed technical issues that I didn't understand. His animated hands almost made up for the loss of his two other limbs. *His dream is coming true*, I thought to myself. I looked over at Emily, and saw contentment.

As Wyatt and the crew set up his gear, tiny drops of water began to fall from the heavens.

"Feeling a strange mixture of overwhelming excitement and anxiety that I'm about to attempt to DJ Glastonbury Festival…while disabled…in potentially awful weather. Definitely wish I had about at least two more working legs at the moment, but grateful that I'll at least get to attempt this with some of the most amazing people I've ever gotten to call friends."

– Wyatt, social media posting, June 27, 2014

# Thunder and Lightening

*June 27, 2014 * Pilton, Somerset, England*

One of the new friends Wyatt had made during the tour was a well-known German DJ. Looking skyward at an approaching storm she quoted Queen's Bohemian Rhapsody in accented English, "Thunder and lightning, very very frightening."

We glanced to the west and could see it too. Electricity had begun to illuminate thick black clouds on the horizon. They were followed a moment later by a crackle. I counted aloud after the next bolt: "One, two, three, four, five"… boom.

I waited for the next one. This time I was only able to count to four before the thunder arrived.

"It's getting closer," deduced his DJ friend as she was about to take the stage.

In the distance, a band over at the Pyramid Stage pounded out heavy metal as Wyatt's brow furrowed, "Looking pretty ugly up there." Though performers were covered, fans were not, and they were almost as important to him as friends and family were.

As his DJ friend went up on stage, Wyatt told her to "shred the dance floor." She scaled the steep stairs and I was thankful that Wyatt's agent and manager had already offered to carry him up in his wheelchair when it was time for his own set.

During the German girl's show, several hundred fans celebrated her tunes by bopping, shuffling, gliding, and jumping. Wyatt tried to enjoy her show too, but I noticed him glance at the sky more than once as the lightening intensified and the thunder became louder and closer.

"Looks ugly," Emily said to me, no longer interested in what was happening on stage.

The German DJ managed to get through her one hour set before it was time to launch the ark. As she came down from the stage, the last thing I heard Wyatt say to her was "Big ups. That was amazing!"

That's when the deluge started and hurricane force winds pounded the area. A mile away from us a tree burnt to the ground after lightning struck it.

*****

In a panic, tens of thousands of people scurried about the grounds trying to get out of the storm. All of Glastonbury's stages had gone dark as the performers dashed for cover in the sheltered areas just behind them. The risk of having their stars electrocuted by the lightning forced the organizers of the festival to cut short and out-right cancel all of the shows scheduled for the next few hours. Only a few times in its history had they taken such drastic measures.

"That's okay," Wyatt said, undaunted. "It's alright. There's still tomorrow. That's the really sweet gig anyway."

# Journey to Glastonbury

As he sat in his wheelchair, staring outside the backstage area at the flooding and fire coming from the sky, Wyatt's imagination took hold of him. He saw himself on the Hell Stage tomorrow night, thousands of fans huddled shoulder-to-shoulder with their fists pumping in the air and celebrating as he spun his tunes. In his mind's eye he could hear the crowd, as his most popular production, "Ready, Set, Party" played in his head.

*****

As darkness enveloped the festival, the wind and rain died down enough for me to wheel Wyatt back to the place where we could catch a taxi to our hotel in Bristol. Pushing him was so much harder this time, and it wasn't just because of the beige colored mud that the wheels were sinking in.

Emily walked behind us, eyes cast downward under her hood.

# A Bridge to Nowhere

*June 28, 2014 * Bristol, England*

"Is Wyatt with you?" Emily asked me the next day after knocking on my door.

"I thought he was with you," I answered.

"Well, he's not. He was talking to someone on the hotel phone, and the next thing I heard was the door closing. I'm not even sure how he was able to get out of the room; he's having a hard time getting around in his wheelchair."

"He must be in the lobby, or the restaurant." We looked at each other for a moment as I watched the concern grow in her eyes. Together we headed for the elevator.

He was not in either of those places, nor was he in the lounge or the gift shop. There was a spa in the basement, so Emily checked there while I looked in the fitness center and then the men's room.

"Wyatt's not in the hotel." Emily concluded. "He's just not here. This is so unlike him."

I asked the front desk clerk if he'd seen him. "Oh, yes." The polite young man in a dark suit and red tie answered. "I saw him roll out about twenty minutes ago. He had a hard time with the door, and when the valet tried to help him he was yelled at." He frowned as he related this last part.

Emily said, "Something's wrong. I wish he had a cell phone."

"I'll go out and look for him," I offered, "You go up to the room and wait for him. If he shows up, text me."

Wyatt had been in a wheel chair for less than a week. He was not used to pushing himself in it, so he couldn't have gone far. As I exited the hotel, I looked to the right. There was an aquarium there, and a little further down, a riverside park. In the other direction was another park, this one closer. I walked down the staircase, noticing the ramp he would've used, and turned left.

Fifty yards into my trek, I was already soaked from the rain that had not stopped falling since the epic storm of yesterday. That's when I saw the two towers of the Bristol Cathedral jutting up into the soot colored sky. The entrance was not far from where I now stood. Wyatt's not a religious guy, but I decided that I should still check it out.

The cathedral had been built in the twelfth century - we had heard during an open-air bus tour - with most of it finished in the fourteenth. I think the guide had said it was gothic style. As I entered, I could hear music coming from the grand pipe organ that stood in the middle. I searched the Eastern Lady Chapel, the Berkeley Chapel, and finally the Elder Lady Chapel, but he wasn't in any of them.

I checked my phone to see if Emily had texted me. Finding it clear I walked back to the hotel entrance and continued past it to the aquarium. He wasn't there either. A hundred yards further in this direction was the other park, one that we had visited a few weeks earlier. As the rain continued to pelt me, I decided that this seemed like a good place to look.

I arrived at the park and walked down a path towards the Avon River. That's where I found him.

Wyatt was sitting in his chair in the middle of a winding pedestrian bridge. The wet tires glistened, and looked bigger than they really were. He was looking down at the river through the glass sides. A few mallard ducks floated by, while drops of rain splashed all over the water's surface.

I hurried toward him, pulling my phone out to let Emily know that I'd found him and that I'd call her back.

As I approached I could see that his Skid Row Records jacket was drenched and his hair matted and dripping. Tears had streaked his face so recently that they hadn't been washed away by the weather.

"Wyatt. What is it? What's wrong?" I yelled over the patter.

He looked over at me, his dark hazel eyes rimmed with red. For a long moment, he just sat there until finally he began to speak, so quiet that I barely heard him, "When they told me that I was going to die, I rolled with it. I really did." I nodded, because it was true, he had remained positive throughout his ordeal. He continued, a little louder this time, "Then this stupid wheelchair thing. I rolled with that too, all the way here… all the way to Glastonbury, ten

142

thousand miles away from home - just because I want to matter. I want my life to matter. I want to have done something with it, something special, and to be remembered… *if...*"

His voice trailed off and he focused on the ducks below. When he spoke again his voice was louder and just a little angry, "Then along comes the 'storm of the century', burning down trees and raining out my show yesterday."

I waited for him to continue, but he didn't. Then I tried to encourage him, "It's okay, Wyatt. Thankfully, you've still got that gig tonight, at Glastonbury's Hell Stage."

He reacted as if he'd been struck, and gasped for air. That's when his eyes welled up and began to overflow with a new trail of tears running down both cheeks.

I thought about the phone call he had received back at the hotel.

*****

The call had been from Wyatt's manager.

"I'm afraid that I've got some rather unfortunate news for you," He told Wyatt, his voice without emotion, "The promoter of tonight's gig at the Hell Stage has canceled your performance. He heard that you couldn't even walk anymore, so you can't put on a proper show. I'm sorry mate it's out of my hands." Even though he knew what this news would do to Wyatt, he hadn't had the decency to tell him in person, though his office was only a short distance from the hotel.

"They can't do that, there are laws protecting disabled people," Wyatt complained, though he knew nothing of English law. "Aren't there?"

The response was cold and final, "I tried to get him to change his mind, there's nothing more I can do, I'm sorry. I have to go now mate, cheers."

It was at that moment that Wyatt realized that his manager had abandoned him. He became dizzy and felt sick, as he began to mourn a dream that had just died.

He slammed the phone down and maneuvered his wheelchair out the door, desperate for air.

# Ibiza, a Year Earlier

*\* Summer, 2013 \* an island off the eastern shore of Spain*

Jean-Paul was already a famous DJ by the time Wyatt had even seen his first electronica concert. Over the years, he had become one of the best-known turntablists in all of Europe, with thousands of adoring fans. One of the drawbacks of his career was the non-stop world travel it required – today he was the main attraction at a dance music festival on the Mediterranean party island of Ibiza.

Hours before his show he sat at a bar reading a music production magazine he had picked up at the airport in Milan. This was his first introduction to Lewd Behavior. The article read,

> "So young and so talented! Rising star Lewd Behavior (known to his mum as Wyatt) has been making waves in the breaks scene with props from dance heavy weights Diplo, Stanton Warriors, and Daddy G of Massive Attack. Is it any wonder with tracks like *Ready, Set, Party*, exercising the finest in throbbing, squelch synths, hard hitting break beats and hip-hop vocals? This 20 year-old is clearly going places."

Jean-Paul put his headphones on and searched the internet for the young music producer's work. As he sipped his beer and listened to Lewd's tunes, his toes were tapping. "Good stuff," he muttered. Several of them would become staples of his shows over the next year.

145

# Cheddar Gorge

*\* June 5, 2014 \* Southern England*

Almost a year later, during Wyatt's UK tour, the two finally met at an event in which they shared the bill. On that Friday, Wyatt admired the established DJ's work, while the next day it was Jean-Paul's turn to admire his young protégé's talent. Over beers afterward, they talked about new technology, synths, and some of the people they both knew in the industry.

"Hey Em," Wyatt said as she returned to their table where the two of them sat with broad smiles on their faces. "Jean-Paul just invited us to tour Cheddar Gorge with him tomorrow. What do you figure?" She of course was elated to do something touristy, so she quickly accepted the invitation to this natural wonder twenty miles south of Bristol.

The next day the three of them explored the craggy limestone walls that lined both sides of the steep gorge, and enjoyed an ice cream along the way.

"That's Gough's Cave over there," Jean-Paul said pointing further down the road to a modern two-story building attached to the face of a jagged cliff. As Emily took a step forward, Wyatt craned his neck to get a glimpse of it while still perched on his crutches. "A ten thousand year old human skeleton was found in there. Murdered by cannibals I reckon."

# The Last Day of Glastonbury

*9:37 am * June 29, 2014 * Pilton, Somerset, England*

Jean-Paul was a staple of the Glastonbury Festival, this year being the fifth time he had been invited to perform there. He was slated to play the Hell Stage, though his show was on Friday night, and canceled by the same storm that put the kibosh on Wyatt's performance. On Saturday, while Wyatt was supposed to be doing his second show, Jean-Paul performed on a different stage. On Sunday, he had one last gig at a nightclub in the center of Glastonbury Festival.

Spontaneity was one of Jean-Paul's traits. He woke up in his luxury tent on Sunday morning, earlier than usual, and had an epiphany. Wyatt's strength was mixing and producing sweet EDM tunes, while his was beat juggling and scratching. It dawned on him that the two could put on a hell of a show together.

# The Phone Call

*9:55 am * June 29, 2014 * Bristol, England*

There were two things that Jean-Paul didn't know when he called Wyatt that morning. The first was that both of his shows at Glastonbury had been canceled.

"What do you say bro?" Jean-Paul asked after offering him the chance to perform back-to-back at the festival that evening.

"I guess you haven't heard?" Wyatt replied.

Over the past 24 hours, Wyatt had tried desperately to stay positive and hopeful about his future, but the partially filled suitcases on his bed and the return flight itinerary on the desk mocked him. In the garbage next to him was the official Glastonbury Programme he had received on his first day at the festival. Lewd Behavior was listed on page 48.

"It's going be awesome, Dude. We'll kill that dance floor together. Last night of Glasto, let's give them something to remember!" Jean-Paul said, talking over Wyatt and almost missing the question. He suddenly stopped talking, "Heard what?"

There was no hesitation in Wyatt's voice. "No legs, dude. Can't walk at all. I do have this really sick deluxe wheel chair though, so I can get around, sort of." He let out a chuckle that faded quickly.

Like Wyatt, Jean-Paul was an extrovert and usually happy, but his mood ebbed, "Sorry to hear that mate, what happened? How?"

Wyatt told him how the paralysis had started, but not of the tumor in his spine that had caused it. As he did so, his friend came up with a plan.

"You can still DJ, right?" Jean-Paul asked.

Having had his world crushed not once but twice, Wyatt resisted hope. "Well, yeah. But…"

"What time can you be at the artist's check-in center?"

# A Man from Cornwall

*11:20 am,* * *June 29, 2014 * Pilton, Somerset, England*

At this point in his career, most of Jean-Paul's gigs were concerts and festivals. However, he often missed the intimacy of a small venue where he could be close to people instead of elevated high up on a stage. A few days prior to Glastonbury, when his gray-haired friend Michael asked him if he'd like to perform unannounced at his club located in the middle of the festival late Sunday night, he jumped at the chance.

On Sunday morning, when Jean-Paul phoned Michael to tell him that he had invited a talented up and coming young man to play a set that evening, his friend thought aloud, "This bloke must be really good?"

"Yeah, great producer. He's got a lot of potential." Jean-Paul answered, though the question had been rhetorical.

"Honored to have the two of you at my place tonight."

"Well, yeah. But there's one issue."

"What's that mate?"

"He can't walk at all. He's in a wheel chair," answered Jean Paul, "… had a bad fall about week ago," He assumed it had been a tumble, but he had never actually been told what caused Wyatt's paralysis, though he suspected that it might be something more sinister.

"Not a problem," the Cornish man let out a jolly laugh. "I'll just get my guys to build a ramp for him. I'll even pick him up personally at the artist's entrance and give him the grand tour of Glasto."

# The Last Night of Glasto

In the studio he is meticulous and on stage he is outrageous. His production sonics replicate the noise that a seriously perturbed Godzilla would make rising from the ocean depths. If Lewd Behavior had never heard of drum and bass, you could explain the concept to him, go to bed, wake up eight hours later and he'd be sitting on top of the most jaw dropping pile of drum and bass anthemic glory you would have ever heard.

- A music festival profile of Lewd Behavior

*7:58 pm * June 29, 2014 * Pilton, Somerset, England*

The brightly lit façade of Michael's nightclub illuminated the darkness as we got out of his truck where the four of us had been packed tight on its bench seat. Wyatt's gear had to be stowed in the back, but lucky for us it was a clear starlit night with nary a rain cloud. The place was impossible to miss, unique even among the weirdness that was Glastonbury. The wooden front of the huge tent was a kaleidoscope of colors, with "Rum and Ale" in huge red letters that dominated the smaller blue letters that let patrons know that they had entered the "Cornish Arms."

The sandwich board out front told of ales, lagers, cocktails, and a "fabulous bar staff". There was no mention of anyone performing tonight – it was a secret.

True to what he had told Jean-Paul in the morning, Michael had taken us on a tour of the largest greenfield festival in the world, one square mile dedicated to the performing arts that was called Glastonbury. The highlight was the fifty-ton fire-breathing spider that crawled above the spectators at the Arcadia Stage. He then took us for a beer in the Greenroom behind the main stage where the most famous musicians in the world chilled. The Cornish Arms itself was located out in Left Field; a hundred yards down the road from the Pyramid Stage where Wyatt had heard his favorite band perform on Friday night, a few hours prior to his own rained out show.

As we entered the club, a couple danced to canned music - he bald and dressed for the tropics and she slightly overweight and dressed for the prom. A female friend of theirs, face painted and smile pronounced, stood so close to them that she was almost part of their twirling, though the drink in her hand kept her stationary. The music was so low that it couldn't drown out the din of the patrons, most of whom sat in one of the wooden couches strewn about the place. Plywood covered the grass, and I remembered that during the rest of the year this pasture was part of a working dairy farm. I wondered where all the cows were? In the center of the tent's rooftop hung a crystal ball.

In the hour before the show, Wyatt, Emily and Jean-Paul talked and laughed as they sat at a wooden table near the stage, while I sat at the bar and chatted with Michael about the history of the festival, happy to have someone my own age to talk with. A few minutes after ten, the Cornish man left me and scaled the stairs onto the stage to use the microphone.

"Ladies and gents, all the way from Canada - a young man that the great Jean-Paul says is destined for great things of his own - give it up for Lewd Behavior."

The beer drinkers applauded, and when I looked over at Wyatt, his face shone bright, as if a million fans had just given him a standing ovation. He kicked things off with synthesized bass and drums that pounded the place in a staccato rhythm, as the pre-recorded voices of his two Jamaican friends, who sounded like Bob Marley, announced that we were about to hear the sounds of Lewd Behavior.

As Wyatt's electronic dance music blared at full tilt, Jean-Paul began to scratch, something I had never before witnessed. His hands were so fast they were a blur as he used a special turntable to layer different sounds over Wyatt's productions. The audience, infected by the rhythm, began to sway, and soon afterwards... dance, shuffle, and gyrate... and the place suddenly felt full.

Twenty minutes later the show at the Pyramid Stage ended and it seemed that most of those people had moved over here. The crowd was now shoulder-to-shoulder as they expanded out the open side of the nightclub onto the main thoroughfare, and now they bounced because there wasn't room for anything more.

Wyatt, in his wheelchair, celebrated the music as best he could. His long arms waved back and forth in the air and I could see a toothy grin. Ten feet to his right, Jean-Paul continued to scratch, and I appreciated the sweet, subtle effects he carefully layered over Wyatt's songs.

Forty minutes into the set, Wyatt added my favorite into the mix - a haunting synth-heavy production, light on vocals. It was at that moment that I felt pride for what my son had accomplished.

An hour and half into the set, the crowd had swelled so big that it went further down Glastonbury's mud covered avenue than the eye could see.

Twenty minutes later, the saxophones of Wyatt's final mournful tune bellowed to signal that the show was over. When all was quiet, few seemed to notice what I did. With Wyatt wearing a smile that was brighter than the stage lights, Emily ascended the stairs and hugged him. As she thought of everything Wyatt had gone through over the past year, and how hard this tour had been on the both of them, she crumbled into tears as she realized that Wyatt had done it… he had finally played Glastonbury.

"Can't believe I'm going home tomorrow from my first ever UK tour... Six weeks of AMAZING shows, AMAZING people, AMAZING culture, and so many memories that I'll cherish forever... becoming disabled while on tour was absolutely terrifying, but I'm so grateful to have had the opportunity to make it happen. Thank you to everyone who carried me up onto stages, built ramps, drove me around the mud in my wheelchair, and kept on pushing me to have the very best time that I could possibly have. I will love you guys forever!"

- Wyatt, social media status update

# Happy Birthday

*\* July 21, 2014 \* Victoria, British Columbia, Canada*

The "Art House", located in a trendy part of downtown Victoria, tripled as a tattoo parlor, gallery, and nightclub. It was here that several dozen of Wyatt's friends gathered to celebrate his twenty-second birthday a few weeks after he had returned from the United Kingdom. By this time, his dark hair had grown back rich and full and he now sported a beard. His eyelashes were long, and the eyebrows that he had demonstrated during his display of emotions a few weeks earlier had become thicker. He wore a checkered shirt and jeans, and a backwards ball cap that hid his new locks. Apart from the wheelchair, this was the old happy Wyatt again.

That night his pals raised him and his wheelchair onto the stage where he spun a few tunes, not as Lewd Behavior, but as Wyatt. He had no prepared set; he just played whatever he felt like. Some of the songs were remixes; some were the straight up originals. The one common denominator was rhythm… everything was beyond toe tapping. Everyone danced. Occasionally others had to intervene to keep the tunes going as Wyatt stopped to socialize.

As midnight approached and Wyatt had just finished playing his remix of the Cure's "Just like Heaven", his friends chanted "Wyatt, Wyatt, Wyatt."

When the chant had died down, Wyatt said, "Thanks homies for coming tonight." For a moment, the chant resumed, but it gave way to Wyatt, "As most of you know, I've gone through the craziest roller coaster time of my life." The murmur of the crowd died as his pals realized he had something he wanted to say to them, "Despite all the treatment and chaos, nothing has been crazier than the six weeks I just spent destroying dance floors across the UK. From Shindig Weekender, to Eden Festival to Bassfunk Plymouth to Glastonbury, each event pushed me to my limits physically and emotionally... and it was the raddest adventure I could ever have imagined having. But, best of all, I got to share the experience with the love of my life."

People turned to look at Emily who was talking to a couple of her girlfriend's a short distance away. A slight smile appeared on her face.

"Tell us about Glasto!" someone yelled to the birthday boy. The festival was as mythic to these people as Avalon.

"Well," Wyatt cleared his throat and drank from a glass of water someone had brought him. "As expected, Glastonbury was the most unforgettable weekend of our journey and the absolute most extreme experience of the whole trip. But...", his voice wasn't quite as loud "There was so much anxiety surrounding the show on my part, and even after it all literally completely fell apart at one point, we picked up the pieces and made them fit." He didn't tell them that it had fallen apart twice, nor did he tell them that the conspirators were the weather, music execs, and the lack of two good legs.

He looked at the crowd and sensed they wanted to know more. "I ended up doing a takeover in Leftfield at the

Cornish Arms all night with my party-rocking homie Jean-Paul. The main stage had just closed nearby and so we got a massive rush of people who were eager to hear some good music and drink some good rum. Luckily, we had both covered! Before I played, the festival treated me so amazingly. We got a private tour via artist transport of all these amazing viewing areas and they truly went above and beyond to make sure I checked out the festival and enjoyed myself. Glastonbury, even though it almost didn't happen, happened. It was an unforgettable, lifetime achievement that I'll cherish forever."

His friends resumed the chant, and this time Wyatt raised his hands to quell it, because he had more to say. "Looking back on it, here in Canada, I can't believe we did all that. After all the chemotherapy, the radiation, the doctors, and the pain we've experienced since last year – it's hard to remember that life is out there for us to take on sometimes! We overcame challenges, we persevered through extreme conditions, and we banded together and made things that felt impossible possible again."

Then his voice took on a Shakespearian quality that could have landed him the lead in Hamlet,

"When you fight cancer, it can be hard to deal with how harsh reality can be. But, when you put your mind to amazing things, even in times of turmoil and negativity, you will accomplish your dreams and goals and succeed." He paused for a second and looked from side-to-side at all his dear friends, "If you're up against adversity, I hope you can use my story to inspire you to reach for whatever you love. If you're not, I still hope you can use this to inspire you to reach for your dreams. If you want something, fight hard for it. Be it life, your dreams, your love, or just happiness."

The festive birthday party atmosphere had almost died when Wyatt decided to revive it. "Let's hear some dope new tunes!" He then unleashed a blistering remix of the White Stripes "Fell in Love with a Girl" and his buddies once again danced. The remainder of the night was filled with laughter, celebration, and (of course) good music.

After the party, Wyatt and his closest friends went to a waffle restaurant to cap the celebration. He returned home as dawn approached and slept peacefully on the chaise lounge in their living room with Emily curled up beside him.

# Part Four – Back to Now

*That all happened in the first timeline, the 'old' one - the one that is just a memory now, memories that only I have.*

*What I remember is that Wyatt was sick, he got better, and he went on tour. Just before the most important show of his life, the spread of cancer to his spine paralyzed him. Fighting through this and many other challenges, he played Glastonbury anyway.*

*These memories, good and bad, kept piling up until 2023 when I visited Stonehenge to observe the summer solstice. That's when the clock was rewound, all the way back to January of 2013 – a full six months before Wyatt's illness had even been discovered in that first timeline.*

*A lot happens in the new reality that didn't happen in the first one, and that's where I take you in this next part – to the new timeline... after Stonehenge sent me back.*

# The Australian... Again

*\* January, 2014 \* Victoria, British Columbia, Canada*

On January 7, almost exactly one year after I awoke to this Stonehenge miracle, Wyatt enters the operating room. Over the past nine months, he has had six rounds of harsh chemo, and six weeks radiation treatment. Both have taken a heavy toll on him. Our entire family waits in the lobby for the duration of the six-hour surgery to remove the bone cancer in his hip that has remained tiny compared to what it had been in the old timeline. His mom, Margaret, fiddles with the artificial bouquets on the end tables, her fingers trying to breathe life to the plastic. Older brother Anthony holds a book in his lap but never turns a page. I watch his eyes move mechanically across the same line, over and over. Emily's mom, Peggy, meditates, eyes shut, faintly humming in tune with a wavelength only she can hear. Younger sister Taylor taps furiously on her mobile, legs crossed and one foot twitching.

Emily and I stare straight ahead at the door. I cannot read her face any more than I can read her thoughts. Instead, I turn inward to my own fear, my own relief. As daunting as a surgery sounds to the loved ones around me, this was the beginning of our failing hopes. This surgery was the unattainable dream of that other reality.

...And here we are.

Not for the first time, I feel fervent gratitude for the gift I've been given, the simple chance. Not for the first time, I am knocked breathless when I know that in the end, second chance or not, I may be unable to change the future. It's this feeling that anchors me, that keeps me critically invested in every step of the treatment.

The doors at the end of the room open, knocking me back into the present. "Wyatt?" The Australian surgeon asks, looking for us but not quite remembering what we look like. We are on our feet in a split second, Taylor's phone clattering onto the linoleum without anyone noticing. "The patient is out of surgery." The Aussie smiles, "Everything went fine. He should be awake for visitors very shortly." He turns to Emily, "Do you want to sit with him until he wakes up?"

"Please." We are stopped by the gasped word, the first sound Emily has emitted in hours. Even I am taken aback by her face, drawn and white. She brushes past Peggy's outstretched hand and follows the doctor like a drowning girl seeking air.

*****

The next day we're all back at the hospital.

"I'm telling you, dude, I remember the whole thing," Wyatt insists from his bed, his eyes gleaming.

"That's literally impossible!" Anthony exclaims, but a smile twitches the corners of his mouth. "There's less than a one percent chance of that happening, do you know how powerful the anesthesia is?"

"Not powerful enough, bro." Wyatt sniffs disdain. "I could identify the exact scalpel they used. The nurses were totally checking me out, too, but I told them right before the doctor started slicing that I'm a taken man."

"No you didn't" Emily interjects, knowing Wyatt too well.

"I meant to, but I fell asleep". We all laugh.

"That I believe," replies Emily.

A sly smile appears on Wyatt's face. "You know what I should've done?" We shrug, and he continues, "I should have tattooed my tour dates onto my thigh, like free advertising! 'Lewd Behavior's European Tour, coming this June!' It's finally happening!"

# Redux

Just as they had in that first reality, Wyatt's record company set up an international tour for him beginning in June of 2014. In this second life after the pillars of Stonehenge rewound the clock, Lewd Behavior once again performs in Scotland and England, as well as in Italy and France.

We are constantly on the go. A day at the Bristol Zoo is the only tourist activity we have time for. I can tell that the pace of this is wearing on the usually happy couple. They are getting snippy with each other, and occasionally with me as well. I understand the tour's intensity; the promoter is trying to make as much money as possible. The only way he can do that is to keep Wyatt (aka Lewd) constantly working. Before this, Wyatt had never performed more than twice in a week. In one seven-day stretch of this tour, he performs five times, in three different countries.

His impending performance at Glastonbury sustains him, just as it did during the harshest moments of his cancer treatment in that first timeframe. When the tour logistics disheartened him, he just thought of taking the stage at the iconic music festival and he was happy again.

# A Proposal

*11:42am * June 18, 2014 * Bristol, United Kingdom*

In this new *post-Stonehenge* world, this is the day that events begin to diverge in a big way from what they had been in the old timeline.

*****

"Hey, Pops." Wyatt appears at my open hotel room door, "Feel like a pint?" Normally he would say beer, brewski or suds, but here in the UK it had become "pint".

"Where's Emily?" I ask, suspicious of the offer. He's taken aback at the insinuation that he only wants to hang out with me because his soul mate isn't available.

"I have something important I want to talk to you about, alone," Wyatt replies. I raise an eyebrow at him and he flashes his almost perpetual smile – the one that never faded in that old timeline even when things got so bad. "Emily's at the spa. Getting a cucumber-something-or-other. But still, I honestly want to hang out with you… and I have something important I want to talk about."

Looking at him with furrowed brow I reply, "Alright, then, lunch and a pint?"

"Awesome, I'm starving."

We find ourselves in the elegant vintage chairs of a nearby pub, with sleek wood paneling and the exposed stone of the walls telling us that this place is old. On a square tube-style television mounted high up above us, two teams are playing cricket.

"What can I get you, love," says a mature jean wearing barmaid with a cockney accent. After we give her our orders, I thank her and she responds, "No worries."

Our chitchat is mundane at first, lasting until only crumbs are left. As Wyatt wipes the corner of his mouth with a napkin he says, "Pops, I have something important to say." He takes a deep breath and I try not to panic, immediately on high alert from the gravity in his voice. "Emily and I have been together for a long time." What he says after his brief pause shouldn't surprise me, but it does. "I want to propose to her."

"You... what?"

"Dude, just hear me out," he insists with a chuckle, as though I have spoken against him. "I know we're young, but I can't imagine ever loving someone more. Dad, being diagnosed with cancer," he meets my eyes, one of the rare occasions he'll directly mention the diagnosis, "the treatment, the fear, the anger at the world and sometimes at each other. It's taught me so much." As he says this, I think back to that old world when his illness and treatment were so much worse, a world he still knows nothing about. He continues, breaking my reverie, "I could never love anyone more than I love Emily. I want to grow old with her, Dad." He pauses, seeing his future life play out in his mind.

Finally, Wyatt says, *"I thought Glastonbury was my dream, but really... she is."*

I'm silent, sudden and painful memories pressing behind my eyes. The thought of a proposal, if and when it had occurred to him, had been quickly dashed by his failing health. This was a second chance. This was hope.

"Wyatt," I clear my throat, he can see the shine in my eyes. "Emily is an incredible gal, and you two have been inseparable for so long, for over five years already."

Wyatt beams. "I think we're going to need another beer, Daddio."

After re-ordering, we sit silently for a few minutes trying to understand the cricketeers on TV. When the barmaid arrives with our glasses, we're no wiser to this foreign game. I give up and raise my mug, "Cheers to you, Wyatt. To Emily. To both of you." He clinks against it, and we drink.

"Get a load of my plan," he says enthusiastically. "I'm going to propose on stage at Glasto. Before my final number, I'm going to call her from the wings and go down on one knee. It's going to be incredible."

I'm aghast. "Are you nuts? At Glastonbury? In public? On stage, in front of all those people?" I'm mortified, and I know Emily will be too. Wyatt is not prone to harebrained schemes, but here is a rare one. My job is clear: I must talk him out of it.

"Yeah." He nods. Though I can see he's already re-evaluating his plan, "I thought it would be romantic."

We debate his idea for the next ten minutes and soon he has a new one. The time and place is still the same - at Glastonbury. My excitement feeds off Wyatt's as we begin to search for a near-by jewelry store using the map on my phone.

# Emerald

*1:49 pm * June 18, 2014 * in the new timeline*

*Bristol, United Kingdom*

According to the GPS guided map on my phone, we are halfway to our destination when we pass the town's cathedral, its two gothic towers rising high into the air. "We should check it out sometime," I suggest, offhandedly. Wyatt dismisses the notion. If a wedding isn't involved, he's not interested right now.

We have just rounded the cathedral when directly in front of us, as though set there by providence, is an antique shop, its windows filled with jewelry. It's not the one we were on our way to visit.

"Dad," Wyatt's head snaps back as he studies the shop, "I don't think we need to go any further."

The interior is dark and elegant, handcrafted necklaces, earrings, and rings heralding their histories, filling the air with the stories of the people who wore them years ago. Gold, precious stones, and diamonds rest on crushed velvet.

"Can I help you, gentlemen?" The shopkeeper is a slender woman, her hair gray but her face unwrinkled, regal. According to her long gray dress, she was transported to our world from the Victorian era.

"I'm looking for an engagement ring," Wyatt explains, "for the most incredible gal in the world. She's strong, and beautiful, and she loves antiques."

The woman smiles, her eyes bright. "Sounds like everything you could hope for in a wife," she lilts. "It's a good thing you're tying her down, laddie."

Between the two of them, it doesn't take very long for Wyatt to find what he wants. The same way it seems we were guided to the shop, the ring almost finds him. At the center of it is a green emerald, almost as bright as Emily's eyes, a smaller diamond on either side, set in twenty-carat gold. It is perfect, with a price that is within his budget, paid for by the money he's earned so far on this tour. He leaves the shop with the ring in a small white paper bag.

I worry that he'll lose it.

# The Long Journey Home

*\*July 1, 2014 \* the sky over Canada*

The ten-hour flight home feels like twenty. Having crawled from Glastonbury to London's Heathrow Airport, we are now on the transatlantic flight home.

"Flight attendants, please be seated for arrival," says the captain over the plane's intercom.

Sitting behind them, I can see Wyatt looking over Emily at the vista of home through her window. He has to squint because the sun is blinding as it reflects off the ocean. There is no happiness in Wyatt's eyes, just defeat. The happiest guy on the planet can't withstand the sting of what happened just a few days ago. He's thinking about the birthday party that his friends are throwing him in just a few weeks. What will he say to them? This was to be his finest hour, at least to this point in his young life, but instead he feels like a failure.

Emily is also looking out the window, empathy etched on her quiet face. Wyatt looks down at her left hand and his heart sinks. The emerald ring is not on her finger.

*****

*Four days earlier* at Totem Gardens, Glastonbury Festival:

I feel a few raindrops, and the wind picks up. I think back to the last time we were here, in a different life and under different circumstances... and without a ring. I should've

174

been able to predict this storm. Just then, the wind whips into a gale, and the clouds begin to unload their contents by the bucket. Emily and I, and everyone else at the festival, are on the run holding our hats on to keep from getting drenched. The two of us arrive backstage, where Wyatt is still working on his set. Just above us, a flash illuminates the darkening sky, followed by a loud boom a split second later.

*****

Things did not improve for Wyatt that weekend, and Jean-Paul never rescues him.

In the Stonehenge version of life, Wyatt never performs at Glastonbury, and a ring stays in his pocket.

# Christmas Present

On Christmas Day of 2014, in the life *after* Stonehenge rewound the clock, Wyatt meets his new four-legged best friend – a baby golden retriever. He has no recollection of having had this dog before, in the life that only I remember.

In this new timeline, I had made the decision to reunite these two.

*****

On a stealthy yuletide morning, I bring the puppy up to Wyatt and Emily's place. I texted Emily that I was on my way over and she left the door unlocked. After giving the golden fur ball a potty break outside, I enter and place the curious canine on the kitchen floor allowing her to wander freely. The couple is in the living room, with the sounds of Bing Crosby complaining about a lack of snow on an old turntable surrounded by festive decorations, most antique or at least collectible.

"Merry Christmas," I say.

They wish me the same, the little creature nowhere in sight. The door to the bedroom is closed, and there is nothing at risk in the kitchen, so I wait.

"What did you get for Christmas?" I ask Emily.

"Wyatt got me this beautiful necklace." I immediately recognize it. It is the same one he bought her two Christmas' ago in that other life.

"Nice!"

Still no fur ball.

I saunter into the other room to see what's up. There she is, asleep where I left her.

This is no time to goof off!

I pick her up and give her a cuddle, then put her back on the floor with a push towards the living room entrance. With a wobble, she continues to walk.

Wyatt is too busy examining the new mixing headphones he has received from Emily. She and I look at the pup and then at each other with a knowing smile. With her eyes still on me, she says just a smidge too loudly "Wyatt, could you take the garbage out?"

He doesn't look up from the headphone's instruction manual. "Garbage day on Christmas? Whatever dude."

"Yes, and I can hear the truck coming." She puts her hand to her ear. "Seriously *dude!*"

He takes the bait. With urgency, that I hope won't cause him to trip over the puppy, Wyatt leaps off the couch ready to get that trash to the curb and once again be Emily's hero. That's when he sees the other "her".

A flashback reminds me of when he had demonstrated the use of eyebrows to convey emotion, when we were in Bristol in that first timeline and he had just noticed that they had grown back. As if he remembers too, his eyebrows furrow as he studies the little dog. Then they rise high up

177

on his forehead as his eyes go from confusion to the dawn of sudden understanding. I almost expect the demonstration to go on as it did back then.

"Seriously, Pops... you. You got me a puppy?" the little golden retriever begins to wag her tail at Wyatt's excitement. "Dad?"

"She's from the entire family, actually." They just don't know about it yet. "It's been a hard year for you, we thought you deserve it." It has been easy comparing to what we went through in that other reality.

He picks her up. "What am I going to call you?" If Wyatt had a tail, it would be wagging too.

"She's Angel," I say. He accepts that the puppy already has a name and never considers changing it. Maybe deep down, he and Emily both knew her name already.

*****

Later that day, as we sit for Christmas dinner at Margaret's house, Wyatt's cell phone rings.

"It's Doctor Markham," he says recognizing the number of the same lady who served as his oncologist in the other version of life. "I guess she wants to wish her favorite patient a merry Christmas." He presses the green button to accept the call, "Yo Doc, I got a puppy!" he says to her without exchanging any greeting. He cradles Angel in his left arm like a football while he balances the phone to his ear with the right. Then in answer to the caller's reply he says "Merry Christmas to you too."

For a second my chest tightens with panic. What had the scans shown this time? As Wyatt puts the puppy on the floor and raises his arms in victory, I realize that my fear is unwarranted.

"Yes! Yes! Yeah!" Wyatt yells with the active cell phone still in his hand. He begins to walk around the room, arms still raised. Then he waves us all in. "Group hug," and we coalesce around him. He returns to the call struggling to free his arms from the mass of people, "Merry Christmas, Doc. We're celebrating. Talk later." He hangs up the phone and turns to us saying in a voice sure to set off car alarms, "I'm completely cured! *Cured*! I am free!"

Angel, new to life, watches with her tail at full wag … and has an accident.

# Part Five – I Remember

*Wyatt was free from cancer in that new timeline, but back here in the old one, he was not. His struggle continued through the end of summer and into the fall. As time marched towards Christmas, each passing day took a little more of Wyatt with it.*

*In this part of the story, we return to Wyatt, in that old remembered life, in the timeline before Stonehenge worked its magic.*

# Once Upon A Time There Was an Angel

*December 25, 2014 * Victoria, British Columbia, Canada*

"Her name is Angel, because I need one right now," Wyatt had said of the puppy in that other life, the one that I remember.

CT scans after Wyatt had returned from the United Kingdom showed that the chemo had failed. Nothing could stop the ceaseless march of what was growing inside him. Thus far, it had spread from his hip, to his lungs, and to his backbone. A month earlier, his upper leg bone had broken by merely adjusting his position on the couch. Furthermore, despite our best hopes, he was destined to live out the rest of his days in a wheelchair.

A week after his twenty-second birthday, an experimental chemo treatment was attempted. It was just as futile as everything that had come before it.

*****

As I entered their place on Christmas Day in that old timeline, a gingerbread house rested on the kitchen table, a product of Wyatt and Emily's engineering the night before. Next to it sat four bottles of pills and next to them a box of the syringes used to inject Wyatt with blood thinners. A nurse visited each morning and night and her logbook sat at the opposite end of the table.

182

"Let's bring it out now," Wyatt's voice was wispy, and had taken on a higher pitch.

I looked over at Emily and she nodded. As she went to the closet in the hallway, I went to their sleeping area where Wyatt now had a hospital bed, and pushed the machine used to hoist Wyatt in and out of it, into the living room where it was to be used to hold up the mystery item.

As Emily arrived with the white snowman and a stick Taylor asked, "What's this?"

"It's a piñata," Wyatt announced. "We totally stuffed it. Emily, Dad, and I packed it full with candy." Then he used an expression I hadn't heard from him since before he became ill. "Let's get cracka-lackin." It was strange to hear him use a term like this in his present condition.

With the snowman shaped piñata dangling from the top of the hoist, we gave the stick to Wyatt. From his wheelchair he took a whack, but his spindly arms were feeble. He took a second swing, and the snowman stood his ground and almost sneered the words "No candy for you." Wyatt couldn't raise his arms for a third attempt.

In the end, Taylor convinced the snowman to rethink its ways. It succumbed to her stick wielding charm and released its precious cargo, which came crashing to the floor. Everyone dived to get their share, while Wyatt looked on from the confines of his chair with a slight grin on his face, holding Angel on his lap.

*****

# Journey to Glastonbury

A few days after Christmas, I was alone with Wyatt and the little yellow fur ball. I took a moment to grab something from the upper closet in the bedroom and forgot to take the dog with me, leaving her and Wyatt alone in the living room. As I stood on a chair with the object in my hands, the golden retriever decided it was time to relieve herself. In front of Wyatt, not more than ten feet away, she proceeded to do just that. Wyatt sat helplessly, yelling "No, Angel ... No, Angel… No!" Yelling, of course, only makes a three-month old puppy more excited.

Seconds later, I arrived at the scene of the crime. I looked at the puddle and was just about to grab some paper towels when I noticed my son's face.

Slumped in his wheelchair, a torrent of tears rolled down Wyatt's cheeks, and his face trembled.

From that moment on, Wyatt's relationship with the puppy became distant. No longer did he take her to sleep with him on the hospital bed, and no longer did he laugh at her antics. As the end of the year approached, he did not want to hold her anymore.

Wyatt needed a real angel.

# Camille's, Take One

*\* The Life **before** Stonehenge Rewound the Clock \**
*Victoria, British Columbia, Canada*

*New Year's Eve, 2014*

"To six years together," Emily said raising a glass of Moet & Chandon champagne, vintage year 2006. Wyatt was only able to raise his a few inches off the table. "I've loved every minute of every day with you, and I don't want it to end," she said in that long ago world where everything was just a memory.

They were at Camille's Restaurant enjoying the French cuisine in the soft candle light while classical music lingered in the background. Wyatt barely spoke, just getting here had robbed him of what little energy he had. He sat in his wheelchair, surrounded by other couples engaged in romantic banter. He wore a button down shirt that Em had purchased for him just that morning, while she wore an exquisite crème colored dress. She had modeled this new purchase for him earlier that afternoon, after trying on a blue one. When she emerged from the bedroom wearing it, he said, "You look so beautiful." She never took it off.

Emily made small circles with her drink, put her left elbow on the table and leaned forward. "Midnight tonight marks six years since you kissed me for the very first time." She said to Wyatt. Then she sat back and reached across the restaurant table to grip his cold hand. He clasped hers weakly. Then she looked at the bubbles in her champagne

185

glass and said. "This last year has been by far the toughest year either of us has ever had to endure." She looked up, and into Wyatt's eyes and he tried to smile back.

For a moment they did not talk, they just looked at each other. He was in his wheelchair wrapped in a blanket, with a hat on his head. Normally the manager would've insisted on proper attire, but she had known of Wyatt's condition in advance. Wyatt looked back at Emily, and then at the red rose flower petals that were strewn about their table. He noticed that the other tables were barren of flora. Then he saw the manager who was standing to his left about twenty feet away. Their eyes locked and she gave him a nod and a smile.

Just then, the waiter approached with two bowls of soup to begin their four-course meal. The young couple began to sip from their spoons.

"This is good." Wyatt said. When their waiter walked past he asked him, "What kind of soup is this? It's really tasty."

"It's a Japanese dish. I'm glad you like it. How about you young lady, what do you think of it?"

"Isn't this supposed to be a French restaurant?" Emily asked with a sly grin on her face. The she conceded, "It's the tastiest soup I've ever had. What is it called?"

"It's called 'dirt soup'," replied the salt-and-pepper haired man in a three-piece suit.

Emily was the first to drop her spoon in the small plate upon which the bowl sat.

The waiter attempted to ease their concern. "It's actually made from burdock root, in a mildly dirty broth. It's not just dirt… good, isn't it?"

Emily nodded, because it was savory, this could not be denied. Wyatt had hardly eaten any of it, not because he didn't like it, but because his appetite had disappeared several days earlier. He toyed with the soup, took a few sips, and smiled at what the man had said. His glass of champagne remained nearly full while Em's was half gone. He looked overtop the candles that separated them and could no longer hear what the waiter said. Emily's red hair was tied in a neat braid, and she wore a brown shawl over top her dress. She had make-up on, something she hadn't put on her face since their last anniversary a year ago when they had gone to Butchart Gardens. He had never seen a more beautiful girl in his entire life - she just kept getting prettier and prettier as the years went by, he thought to himself. Then he thought of how his Glastonbury dream had come true, and with a frown realized that his real dream would not.

Later, as the dessert course arrived, Emily once again raised her glass to make a toast. "Tonight is so amazing. I love you so much." She waited a moment for Wyatt to raise his glass, but when she realized that he was unable to she said, "You are my hero every single day," and tapped hers against his.

# The Hug

And if you see me, smile and maybe give me a hug.
That's important to me too.

– Jim Valvano, coach, NC State basketball

*January 6, 2015*

My phone rang. The voice on the other end was garbled, so I asked, "Who is this?"

I still could not understand the person's reply. The voice was an unfamiliar mumble. I said, "I'm sorry, but I can't understand you."

Emily came on the line. "It's Wyatt. He wants you to come over and give him a hug."

\*\*\*\*\*

Not only did Wyatt want a hug, he wanted a root beer too, so I stopped on the way and bought him one. As I entered the apartment, Wyatt was still in his hospital bed though the sun that seeped through the windows from the west told me it was late afternoon. He had been moved to the living room, because he wanted to be "where people lived". The wheelchair sat empty in the corner.

Wyatt looked at me with big saucer shaped eyes, exaggerated by his gaunt gray face. His usual smile had faded. Oblivious to her master's condition, Angel was next to his bed where she chewed happily on a stuffed animal that might have once resembled a duck in better days.

I placed the soft drink on the kitchen table, approached him, and did my best to give him the hug he had requested. It felt lame, and I cursed my inability to give him the warm embrace he needed. In the past, Wyatt was always the one who did the hugging. His long arms were like the wings of a giant stork wrapping around you - but the warmth resembled that of a panda bear. You enjoyed those embraces, though it had all been Wyatt's doing with little effort required on your part. Today those arms felt like toothpicks, all the flesh gone from them, just bone wrapped in a thin sheath of skin.

I straightened out and left Wyatt watching television while I went into the kitchen to talk to Emily. She stood with her hands on the counter, looking down at the empty sink. "What's going on?" I asked her in a low voice.

She didn't look up. "He started bleeding from a sore on his back. The nurse can't stop it. If she dares to take him out of bed, he'll just keep on bleeding. The pressure of him lying on his back is the only thing ..." She looked up at me and guessed my next question. "He doesn't want to go back to the hospital." Gauging my reaction, she said, "I've been on the phone with the hospice and they have a bed available. That's where he's decided to go. Wyatt just wants to be comfortable. He doesn't want to leave until tomorrow morning – he wants one more night at home."

# The Stars in Heaven

*January 11, 2015*

Wyatt dreamed.

In his dream, he could see his grandfather, the one with whom he had gone fishing and played cribbage. The old man led him on a tour of a strange euphoric place, bright and full of joy. Those who sat by Wyatt's bedside overheard him whisper, "That looks really nice." As the tour of this enchanted place ended, his grandfather told him that they would soon be together here, and that his old fishing buddy would serve as his guide. To this Wyatt answered, "I'm looking forward to it." His voice was barely heard by those who surrounded his bed.

The dream ended and Wyatt found himself thrust back toward consciousness. He wondered how long he had been sleeping. He had no idea what time it was, but the sunlight that entered through the window suggested that it was mid-day. He could see his ginger sitting in a chair next to him, and he could feel the touch of her hand. Tears trickled down from her red-rimmed eyes.

"Why are you crying?" he said in a wispy voice that she could barely hear.

Emily shook her head. "I'm just sad." She tried to force herself to smile.

He didn't have the energy to ask her why she was sad. Instead, he thought about his wish. *I just want to grow old with her*. He knew that it would not happen, at least not in this lifetime. Her voice brought him back.

"How are you doing, Wyatt?" Emily asked.

He gave her a thumbs-up and smiled.

\*\*\*\*\*

*We were meant to grow old together*, Emily thought to herself. The look in Wyatt's eyes told her that he had been thinking about it too. After six years together, their minds had almost become one.

She felt so tired. So many nights spent in the hospital, so many days having to inject him with medication, so much pain. Why had this happened to them? She blamed the food, full of carcinogens. She vowed to become a vegan.

At that moment, Emily noticed that Wyatt had slipped back into a coma, and she suddenly thought of the rooftop garden jutting up toward the sky, and the stars in heaven that would shine above that place tonight.

\*\*\*\*\*

*L-O-V-E*, Margaret thought to herself as she watched Emily holding Wyatt's hand. She saw Wyatt's eyes open briefly, and he had said something to Em that she wasn't able to overhear.

Then her mind drifted to those long ago days when Wyatt was a baby. He had been the fattest baby ever, but so cute and bubbly. He was so fat she thought that he might have some sort of gland problem, but as soon as he started walking it all melted away and he had remained lean ever since.

*****

As Anthony looked at his little brother lying silent and unmoving, he realized that he was looking at his best friend. Though they were four years apart, their bond was strong. They played music together, teamed up in videogames, and… partied. That brought a slight smile to his face.

Partying together was not difficult because all of his friends were also Wyatt's friends. Even when he was very young, Wyatt's charisma drew pals of all ages.

As he looked at Wyatt, his eyes welled up and he left. The pain was more than he could bear.

*****

Yes, Taylor and he had been rivals growing up, but she loved Wyatt. He could always be counted on when things were tough. He had been her protector, and had defended her more than once. Wyatt was also her trusted confidant and advisor, and had helped her through some dark times. She thought about how much she was going to miss him, and for a moment, it knocked the breath out of her.

*****

*He had never been on a horse before*, Peggy thought to herself. When she first met Wyatt, he had been a skinny sixteen-year-old with passion and too much energy. She remembered his first time on Emily's horse and how calm he became in the saddle. He seemed to belong there.

Then she thought about Emily. Over the years, Wyatt had been so good to her daughter - always attentive and protective. She'd had her own vision of the future, a wedding… grandchildren.

*****

"I'd like to have a few moments alone with my son." I said to those gathered around his bedside.

After the last person left, I said to Wyatt, "I'm not sure if you can hear me." He had been in a coma for the last few hours. I heard his labored breath as I looked at him, my vision blurry, "I want you to know that we're all going to be okay."

I took his limp hand, the same one that his soul mate had been holding. "I'll watch over Emily to make sure that she does all right in the world," I nodded, though Wyatt could not see. "I'll make sure that she's okay."

*****

As the others had come back into the room, Emily went back to Wyatt's side. She held his hand once again and hoped he would return her grasp. He did not. She tried harder, and pulled his hand toward her, clasped it with both hands this time - as if she could hold him here in our world.

A short while later, she sensed the moment that he left us, and ran out of the room with tears streaming down both cheeks.

# The Soul

*January 11, 2015*

*9:11 pm*

As her daughter ran out of the room, Peggy looked over at Wyatt's still form and felt unfathomable grief as she realized she would never talk with him again.

However, she didn't linger in that grief. She got out of her chair and rounded the corner just as Emily pushed through the double doors leading to the stairwell that would carry her to the rooftop garden. In her mind, Peggy had imagined this moment a dozen times, and now it unfolded in a completely different way. She had thought that her daughter would be calm and collected like she had been her whole life, as she had displayed throughout this whole ordeal.

Peggy wished her legs were longer so that she could take the stairs two at time. She thought of the traffic she had heard far below the rooftop garden just the day before, and of the bell Wyatt had rung for his grandfather. She finally reached the top, and burst through the entrance into the garden. She looked around her, and then noticed the nighttime sky above. Rare for this time of year, the sky had opened up and received Wyatt, with not a cloud in the night above, just the endless stars of the universe. Despite the light of the city, she could see the faint outline of the Milky Way and Venus dominating the vista without any moon to overpower them. She observed all of this in less than a

198

second. She wasted no time trying to find the Big Dipper as she went left to look for her daughter.

Not finding Emily in that direction, Peggy circled back... past the doors and the vine-covered trellis. That's when she saw Emily. She had leaned herself against the waist-high fence that kept people from falling over the edge of the roof, and her eyes were fixed on the traffic five stories below.

Peggy slowly approached her daughter. As she came within a few feet of her, Emily gazed up towards the stars and Peggy realized why she had come to this spot - it was because she felt closer to heaven.

In the dim light of a single murky bulb that illuminated that part of the rooftop, Peggy could see Emily's pale face and her glassy eyes that she knew were green.

"Em?" she said gently, but her daughter seemed to be in her own world, not aware that her mother was even there.

Then, Emily calmly walked away. For a moment, Peggy stood there alone until finally she followed. She heard the ringing sound of the bell before she saw Em again. She went to where she knew the sound had come from and saw her daughter with her face pointed skywards, one hand still on the clapper. As Peggy moved forward, Emily's loud voice stopped her in her tracks.

"Bye, Wyatt! Bye!" she waved with her free hand and suddenly looked like a little girl to her mother. "Bye, I love you." She continued waving to a departing soul that only she could see,

As if Wyatt had answered her, the words echoed off the surrounding buildings. "Bye… I love you." A single teardrop glistened as it fell to the ground from Emily's face.

# Part Six – After Stonehenge

*Everything in the last part of the story occurred in the past, in that old life, in that first timeline before the summer sun of Stonehenge transported me back to relive it all over again.*

*Those are just memories—which only I have.*

*...and now, we are back in the present, rewriting the story.*

In this new timeline, after Stonehenge rewound the clock, we catch the cancer six months earlier, and Wyatt learns on Christmas Day, 2014, that he is free of the disease.

*...and a story that never existed in the old world, unfolds in the new one.*

# Camille's *Again*

*December 31, 2014*

Emily walks to the restaurant with Wyatt by her side. He has a long, slow, gliding stride, while hers is short and swift. Their hands are joined, making it impossible for them to become separated.

Inside Camille's, they celebrate their sixth anniversary, just one week after having been told by Doctor Markham that Wyatt is cured.

For the young couple of course, this is their first time here, with no memory of their past life.

*****

As Emily sits in the same chair she had that first time when Wyatt had sat across from her in a wheelchair, the hostess delivers two pre-filled champagne glasses.

"Oh … nice," Em says.

"To the dopest, most awesomest, coolest girl in the world" Wyatt says, unusually excited, and a sparkle in his eye. He raises his glass, "and the prettiest."

Tonight, Emily is wearing the exact same crème colored dress and brown shawl that she had worn in that old life, her red hair once again tied in a braid. She raises her glass while looking into Wyatt's eyes, her face slightly angled and one eyebrow lifted. She taps the glass to his and puts the chalice to her lips. The look on Wyatt's face stops her from taking a sip. "What?" she asks.

With his eyes fixed on her glass, she holds it up to the candle light, and abruptly puts it down.

"Seriously dude!" she laughs in a subtle and very lady like manner - not too haughty, and of course, always under control. "How am I supposed to get that out?"

Just then, the hostess shows up with a long hooked kitchen utensil to save the day. Wyatt takes Emily's glass, and fishes out the dripping object. Then he holds it in his palm extended across the table in front of her, the green glint of the emerald surrounded by tiny white diamonds soaking up the candlelight. He saves her the spectacle of getting down on one knee in front of her, and says, "Will you marry me?" as his hazel eyes look into her green ones.

*****

They have the same dinner as the last time, including the appetizer of dirt soup. Emily has a custom made vegetarian entrée, and Wyatt the duck. Soon they will both be vegan. Toward the end of their evening there is a dessert tray brought over and they choose to share the creme brule.

While Emily's ring finger twinkles with the same color as her eyes, they drink champagne together in the glow.

# Ten Years Later

*September 28,* **2024** *\* Victoria, British Columbia, Canada*

This morning, I am on my way to see my beautiful little granddaughter…Wyatt and Emily's only child. She's four now, and a joy despite having inherited Wyatt's hyper energy level. As I pull up in front of their modest home in a cute area of town, I experience the fear that haunts me all too often – the fear that all of this will vanish and I'll be returned to the old world.

I park my car on the street. It's a sunny mid-September day. The subtle hint that fall is on the way is spread amongst the oaks, maples, and elms. It's Saturday, so Wyatt is at home. After a few years of chasing his musical dreams, playing all over the world as Lewd Behavior, he eventually tired of the travel. Glastonbury, in that other remembered life, turned out to be the pinnacle of his career. In this life, he didn't even get to perform there.

Instead, Wyatt finished his education and was able to land a good job with a local company. Rarely does he spend a night away from the woman and child that are his whole world. He is now 32.

As I get out of my car, walk up the three steps of his front stoop and ring the doorbell, I can hear a commotion inside. It's my granddaughter; she's excited because Grandpa is here. At last, the door opens, revealing Wyatt - still tall, lean and handsome. He's holding someone precious.

He opens the screen door and I exclaim, "Anna-Banana!"

"Popsa!" She giggles, knowing we're going to have nothing but fun. It's Wyatt and Emily's job to mold her into a polite, hardworking, well-behaved young lady. I'm just here to spoil her. Of course, little Anna-Banana always steals all of the attention because she's the most adorable little redhead on earth. Actually, she's the cutest little girl with any hair color. She's such an attention stealer that a golden haired four-legged beauty can't compete. However, Angel gave up long ago, and now the old dog loves to sleep and get a little affection now and then. She doesn't have the boundless energy she had just a few years earlier. She's a little chubby, just like me. With a slow wag of the tail, she saunters up and cuddles by my leg as I sit on the couch.

Their house is less than a thousand square feet, but as quaint as anything in a magazine, due to Emily's decorating prowess. For a moment, I study Wyatt - hardworking like me, as reliable as his grandfather, and more loyal than anyone I have ever known. His beard is manicured now, his hairline slightly receded, but there is no hint of gray in his chestnut hair. His laugh lines are starting to become pronounced. (How could he avoid it? -- he smiles almost all the time).

"Where's Emily?" I ask.

"She's just out with her mom, shopping I think."

As we sit in their tiny living room, I ask Wyatt "What would a good son do?" This was a kind of a running gag when he was a child and after so many years, the answer was well established. Today though, the routine changes. Wyatt turns to Annie and asks, "What would a good granddaughter do?" Her face lights up and she runs to the fridge, bringing back a can of beer for her old granddad. Wyatt and I laugh along with her. Then I say to the munchkin, "What would a good daughter do?" and she excitedly runs to get Wyatt a beer, too. We laugh even harder. Is this child exploitation? No. It's part of being a family and laughing together. When she is old enough to have a beer she will probably say, "What would a good granddad do?" and I will push my walker as fast as I can to get her one… because I love her.

"A toast to Anna-Banana!" I say, and there is a hollow thunk as my can makes contact with Wyatt's. The petite redhead giggles. We sip our beers while Annie settles into making a house out of Lego as Wyatt and I watch with complete and total adoration.

Life is perfect.

Though I'm grateful to Stonehenge, I will never visit it again. I don't dare risk being sent to a timeline that may not be so perfect or worse yet to that old life filled with grief and despair.

To this day, I have not told anyone about what happened, including Wyatt. I don't dare tell him that I lived a life where he died a horrible death and never got to live out his true dream - to grow old with Emily.

# Epilogue

A wife who loses a husband is called a widow.
A husband who loses a wife is called a widower.
A child who loses his parents is called an orphan.
There is no word for a parent who loses a child.
That's how awful the loss is.

- Jay Neugeboren, "An Orphan's Tale"

It is so simple.

Just let me go back to January of 2013 to give me a fighting chance to save my son. Is that too much to ask of the universe?

Of course, the story of how I saved Wyatt is pure fiction, but Wyatt himself…he was real, and so was his death from bone cancer. During his illness, he really did go on tour to the United Kingdom in the persona of "Lewd Behavior", and the cancer paralyzed him just before his gig at Glasto. In the true story, he did the tour with the girl he loved by his side, and performed for the final time from a wheelchair…at Glastonbury Festival of the Performing Arts, on June 29, 2014.

When your child dies, you will do anything to bring them back. The solution to the problem seems so simple – give every parent one chance to alter the past.

Unable to fathom a world without Wyatt, I began writing this book on the night he died as a way to cope with the grief and to keep him alive…for in my writing *Wyatt is alive* and I continue his life story.

Now this, dear reader, is where you get off. From here on it's just Wyatt and me, as I write about his long life made possible by altering one terrible truth – no one can change what has already happened.

*The End*

*"When you put your mind to amazing things, even in times of turmoil and negativity, you will accomplish your dreams and goals and succeed. If you're up against adversity, I hope you can use my story to inspire you to reach for whatever you love. If you're not, I still hope you can use this to inspire you to reach for your dreams. If you want something, fight hard for it. Be it life, your dreams, your love, or just happiness."*

-    *Wyatt, unfinished YouTube video.*

# Acknowledgements

I gratefully acknowledge the contributions of three people who spent many hours editing this book: AMC, Holly Hayton, and Paula Pisani.

I also acknowledge the contributions of the following people who provided input and helped improve this story: Toby Carlos, Tara Panrucker, the TC's, A. Smiddy, Olive (Dea), Haley Perry, Jean-Marc (JFB), and Sammy Senior.

Cover artwork and design by Sparkie Cathcart.

# **About the Author**

Lawrence Compagna was born on Friday the 13th on a brisk winter day in Cold Lake, Canada. Ignoring superstition he chooses to live his life as if it is lucky, traveling the world with pen in hand. He lives in Southern California and British Columbia. Visit the author's Facebook page at fb.me/LawrenceCompagna, and blog at Compagna.xyz

Write to the author at Suite 293, 7582 Las Vegas Blvd S, Las Vegas, Nevada 89123

# Also by the Author

French Canadian Roots

SAP Project Management

*Thanks for reading my book. If you enjoyed it, please rate and review "The Journey to Glastonbury" on websites such as Goodreads, Amazon, Kindle, or in literary publications.*

*- Lawrence Compagna*